W9-AXR-116

THE DEVIL'S DIARIES

Nicholas D. Satan

AS TRANSCRIBED BY

Professor M.J. Weeks

THE LYONS PRESS

ISBN 978-1-59921-408-5

This book was conceived, designed, and produced by
iBall, an imprint of
Ivy Press
The Old Candlemakers
West Street, Lewes
East Sussex, BN7 2NZ, U.K.
www.ivy-group.co.uk

Printed in China

10 9 8 7 6 5 4 3 2 1

Creative Director Peter Bridgewater
Publisher Jason Hook
Editorial Director Caroline Earle
Art Director Sarah Howerd
Senior Project Editor Dominique Page
Designer Clare Barber
Illustrator Suzanne Barrett
Picture Researchers Katie Greenwood, Sarah Skeate
Concept Viv Croot
Concept Design Bernard Higton
Additional Text Viv Croot, Andrew Kirk

PICTURE CREDITS

Akg-images: 67, 84, 90, 99, 104, 106; Johann Brandste: 114; RIA Nowosti: 129.

Bridgeman Art Library/Corpus Christi College, Cambridge, UK: 96R; Prado, Madrid, Spain: 86, 88; Tretyakov Gallery, Moscow, Russia: 12; Whitworth Art Gallery, The University of Manchester, UK: 112.

Corbis: 134, 148, 150, 152; Archivo Iconografico, S.A.: 24, 91; The Art Archive: 45; Bettmann: 5, 16, 75, 98, 103; The Gallery Collection: 69; Greenhalf Photography: 71; John Stringer Collection: 122; Swim Ink 2, LLC: 132.

Getty Images: 121, 140, 154; Frank Driggs Collection: 124; Hulton Archive: 126; Time Life Pictures: 131.

iStockphoto: 26, 119; Christine Balderas: 142L; Hulton Archive: 87; Alex Potemkin: 142R; Steve Ridges: 144; Denise Roup: 109.

Jupiter Images: 10, 33, 43, 55, 56, 58, 61, 64, 65, 76, 77, 82, 93, 96, 100, 107, 118, 120, 127, 135.

Library of Congress, Washington, D.C.: 128.

Rex Features/Images: 142M.

Topfoto: 116; Fortean: 21.

University of Texas Libraries: 73.

PERSONAL DETAILS

Name: Nicholas D. Satan

Home address: The Pentacles, Road to Perdition,

Port au Prince, Haiti

Work address: Satancorp, Level 9,

Ring Road, City of Dis, Hell

Home telephone: 0800 7734-7734

Work telephone: 0800 514-3666 (toll free)

E-mail: oldgoat@evilempire.org

URL: www.evilempire.org

In case of emergency, contact:

Mr. B. L. Z. Bubb, D.A.

c/o Legal Dept.

The Pentagon, Washington D.C.

U.S.A. or

Mr. Mendes Lucifer, L.L.B.

Brimstone, Burns & D'Eath (Solicitors)

221a Baker Street

London, England

My card!

LE DIABLE.

Introduction

During their research academics such as myself have the extreme good fortune to occasionally chance upon truly valuable artifacts or manuscripts. It has been my privilege to make the greatest discovery of all—the long-lost journals of Satan, Prince of Darkness.

These remarkable documents, which span several millennia, first came to my attention during the winter of 2007/8, through a chance encounter with the author's agent. I'd been researching a number of the wilder claims of recent best-selling authors regarding parts of the scriptures supposedly withheld from public view, and found myself in a deconsecrated church in the South of France. While examining a five-pointed mosaic in front of the altar, I cut my finger seriously enough to provoke an impious oath. Luckily for me, I was not (as I had thought) alone; a charming and well-dressed man appeared as if from nowhere, proffering a handkerchief to staunch the bleeding. We fell into conversation and it soon became clear that he was in a position to offer me the chance of a lifetime—to be the only humble scribe permitted to work on the collected writings of the Dark Lord himself.

Following further meetings at the agent's offices in Monte Carlo, I was fortunate enough to gain access to the journals in their entirety. I publish here, for the first time, extracts that confirm what many scholars have only hitherto suspected. This small volume can only present a tiny proportion of the countless entries, but in my selection I have attempted to substantiate the historical significance of the author, and at the same time offer an insight into His extraordinary and charismatic personality.

The present location of the original manuscripts is a closely guarded secret. However, I have left instructions that upon my death ownership shall revert to the author, while my transcript of the contents (on electronic discs kindly supplied by the author's agent) should enter the public domain.

I have taken great pains to establish the provenance of these journals and have no reason to doubt their veracity. Although there are still some who question the existence of their author, I am now convinced beyond any doubt that not only is He a genuine historical figure of immense importance (rather than merely a mythical construct of religious fanatics), but that He is continuing to exert his influence on the world today. Skeptics may question why a harmless academic like me should be accorded the honor of working on these priceless manuscripts: I am unfortunately not at liberty to disclose the details. Suffice it to say that negotiations with the author resulted in a satisfactory agreement surprisingly quickly, and only my signature was required—oddly, in red ink.

MJW
JUNE 6, 2008

M. J. Weeks, MPhil, DivD, OBN
Professor of Comparative Theological Anthropology
University of Milton Parva

Explanatory Notes

Satan had his journals bound in five volumes, reflecting the main epochs of his reign. Volume I is confusingly dated: the first entries predate time and have been retrospectively headed "EBT" (era before time); subsequent entries take as their reference the year zero (calculated by some as Sunday, October 23, 4004 BC), but many have been revised by the author to give the year "BC" ("before catastrophe," referring to the Christian era). Volume II starts with dates marked "AD" ("after disaster"), but soon reverts to standard dating. Where dates are missing, I have attempted to furnish these (in square brackets) with an educated guess, assuming that entries are chronological, and by extrapolating from contemporary sources.

The books are handsomely bound in calf, but the gilt-edged parchment pages have suffered fire damage in addition to the natural ravages of extreme age. Where the manuscript is readily legible, I have reproduced facsimiles, but for most of the text I present my typed transcript—endeavoring to retain the flavor of the original wherever possible—and include any appended memos or memorabilia where these have been salvageable.

Modern imaging techniques have been invaluable in enhancing the diagrams and jottings. Nevertheless, on some occasions, illegibility has necessitated an editorial conjecture (again, in square brackets). Other editorial annotations and footnotes are clearly marked in the text.

MJW

Volume I

Pride Comes Before the Fall

Prehistory and Old Testament:
from the Year <u>zero to</u> 1 BC

[marked "ƐƁƬ," undated]

I, Lucifer, assistant archangel and acknowledged highflyer, one of the brightest and most civil of the servants to the CEO [Consummate and Everlasting Omniscience], have decided to keep a detailed account of my career in the form of a journal. Although I am as yet only a middle-ranking Seraph in the Department of Culture, I do feel I have a lot to offer and am destined for higher things. I am hoping my daily reports will one day chart my rise to high office and prove an example to others.

Me on my first day at the DoC

[marked "EBT," undated]

I've gone through the countless entries since I started this journal and realize I'm not getting anywhere. I've done everything I can to impress The Boss, but He just doesn't want to know—He has surrounded Himself with a bunch of sycophants who simply worship Him and praise every idea He has. It's really difficult working for someone who's both omnipotent and omniscient; we're reduced to pen-pushing desk-jockeys with a negative encouragement scenario vis à vis personal initiative strategies. Frankly, I'm bored to tears. There must be more to life than this. I was told today that I exceeded my job description when I put forward suggestions for hitting the market with a bang and then expanding our operations.

[marked "EBT," undated]

Evicted! Well I'll be ~~damned~~*. Just because He thinks pride is a sin. I suspect it's just jealousy, actually—that Universal Plan of His was just so mundane as it stood, and I stole his thunder with my creative input; His killjoy piety was never any match for my live-wire interventions. Well that's it as far as I'm concerned—no more Mister Nice Guy. Who does He think He is anyway?

[* In the original manuscript this word was heavily crossed out.]

Thought for the day: "Pride comes before the Fall."

[marked "𝔈𝔅𝔗," undated]

And I thought working for Him was dull. Because the CEO hasn't got round to doing anything about His Grand Design yet, there's nowhere to go and nothing to do. It's soul-destroying being unemployed and living in limbo—I wouldn't wish it on my worst enemies. Hang on though … perhaps there's the germ of an idea….

First day, first month, year zero

A busy week ahead, now Mr. High and Mighty has decided to proceed with His "Creation" project. I'll have my work cut out keeping up, and matching big G's inventions with my own. He's already one step ahead: He started early this morning, before I was ready, and created light. I retaliated by creating dark, but it took me most of the day—and I had to stop because I couldn't see a damn thing.

Second day, first month, year zero

God creates a firmament, and calls it "heaven." Exhausted after yesterday, I have a day of rest. Heaven can wait.

Third day, first month, year zero

God divides up "Earth" and "sea"; then He brings forth grass, herbs, and fruit-bearing trees upon the Earth. I create mud, swamps, deserts, and caves; and invent poison ivy and potato blight. Your move, Daddy-o.

Fourth day, first month, year zero

God creates lights in the firmament, to separate light from darkness and to mark days, seasons, and years. I invent night, the dark side of the moon, weather, and the weekend. Touché! (I'm beginning to enjoy this.)

Fifth day, first month, year zero

God creates birds and sea creatures. I counter with a vulture and a few squishy things in the ocean, but my heart's not in it. Have another day of rest.

Sixth day, first month, year zero

God creates animals, then creates Man in His own image and woman from one of Man's ribs, commanding them to be fruitful and multiply. I throw in a few creatures of my own (wasps, slugs, leeches, locusts—that sort of thing), though I have to admit He did a pretty good job with the goats and sloths. Spend the rest of the day thinking about this "fruitful and multiply" thing. Wish I'd thought of it.

Seventh day, first month, year zero

God has a day of rest and sits back to admire His work. I take the opportunity to have a good look around and see where I can best set up business.

Sixth day, sixth month, year Zero

Have at last found premises and should soon be in
business. Builders in (they're crying out for work, now
the Creation project's finished) and refurbishment
underway. A few old colleagues have defected too
(bless them!), so we should be able to show Mr. High
and Mighty a trick or two.
NOTE TO SELF: Organize lively housewarming.

Color scheme? Red and black would be nice....
make a change from that pristine white

Last day, last month, year zero

Building work eventually completed late last night, builders now gainfully (and permanently) employed down in the boiler rooms. But I have to admit they've done a good job. There's a separate level for each department, plenty of accommodations for future residents, and room for expansion. I especially like the security at the gates, with access (and escape!) controlled by the one-way system on the ferry across the river.

First day, first month, year one

It's not easy, running a business like this. Start-up costs are crippling, especially as we haven't yet established a client base. The first fuel bills have just arrived, but the day I pay them is when Hell freezes over! Luckily, the deeds to my estate include mining and mineral rights, so supplies of sulfur, brimstone, etc. won't be a problem in the future. I've already been approached by a company called Helliburton who claim to be experts in extracting profitable material from tricky situations.

UNDERWORLD ENTERPRISES
Now recruiting fallen angels

Fed up with your present job? Dissatisfied with doing good, but not doing well? Opportunities at all levels. Bad employment history or criminal record an advantage, but no previous experience necessary.

Applications, with suitably sycophantic cover letter, to: DEMON RESOURCES DEPT., UNDERWORLD, DIS

Second day, second month, year one

I'm pretty much running on a skeleton staff still, and if I'm serious about building a business empire I'll have to launch a recruitment drive. Career opportunities are pretty good down here, and during Creation week I managed to poach a reliable executive team from contacts in my old job; one of them brought a whole slew of the cheekier of the cherubs with him, and they have already settled nicely into their new role as demons—but I'm going to need a whole host of middle management and admin staff.

Seventh day, second month, year one

An overwhelming response to my ad! And just the sort of dynamic types I'm looking for. Today was especially good—The Boss still insists on a day of rest every seventh day, and everyone knows that idle hands do Lucifer's work. It's something like that anyway....

I've been interviewing all day and allocating tasks for each of the successful applicants (the unsuccessful ones are now helping in the boiler room). A corporate structure is beginning to emerge, with distinct departments on each level of the building and a hierarchy going all the way from vermin, through demons, to myself at the bottom.

How are the fallen mighty!

Eighth day, second month, year one

An interesting meeting with the marketing team. They've been working on a corporate identity for my operations, and came up with some really good ideas. The company uniform of black and blood red is just right I think and projects the image I had in mind— somber, formal, and menacing, not too flashy, but with a dash of color. Still stuck on a logo though: their idea of flames is a little ... well, fussy.

Not too flashy— could become a classic marque

Hmmm ... stretching a point?

Twin arches: a bit obvious?

Keep the cross thing in reserve. May be useful one day

Perhaps the dragon's a bit too cutesy

[a continuation of previous entry]

Some of the new boys have brought livestock with them—mainly rejects from Big G's Creation project—and I'm sure there's potential in biological research. Think of the retail potential if you could develop an eight-legged chicken! I took a tour of the zoological pens this evening and was particularly taken with the goat collected from Mendes. He's a favorite with the keepers, too; they've even given him a name, Baphomet. He really is a handsome creature. Perhaps the logo focus group should come and have a look.

[The Sigil of Baphomet, the symbol of a goat's head enclosed by a five-pointed star within a circle adopted by Satanist cults, was derived from images of the goat of Mendes.]

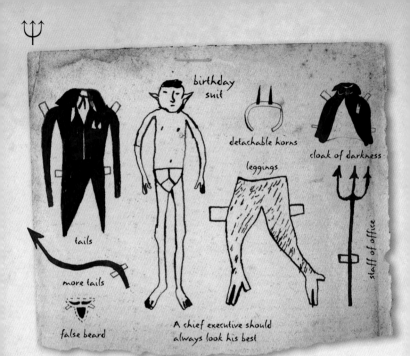

birthday suit

detachable horns

cloak of darkness

leggings

tails

staff of office

more tails

false beard

A chief executive should always look his best

Tenth day, second month, year one

Hell's teeth! My stylists have been working with Marketing and have come up with some ideas for my appearance. I think they've gone a bit too far with the goat thing, but as it was my suggestion I can't refuse. I mean, I like the horns and the beard, and the tail's a masterstroke; but cloven hooves? Not much opportunity for toe-sucking there. I was hoping for something a bit more suave and urbane. The satin-lined cloak is more like it, especially when I'm wearing my tails. And I know it's part of the corporate image, but do I have to carry that pitchfork *all* the time?

[a continuation of previous entry]

What's in a name? Lucifer is the moniker I've always gone by until recently, but close friends also know me as Nick. The staff have to address me as "Most Noble and Magnificent Highness," unless they want a stint in the boiler room, but I know they refer to me as Old Nick behind my back. When I asked my advisors about this, they went into a huddle and tried to come up with something new: "Satan" was top of their list, followed by "The Devil" (a bit feeble, IMHO), and—I think this might be some kind of joke at my expense, but I couldn't figure out how—"Scratch." Well, I don't have to opt for any one, and I might just use all of them, depending on where I manifest myself. Keep them guessing.

Suggested alternatives to Lucifer:

Satan
The Devil
~~Scratch~~
The Dark Lord
Prince of Darkness
Lord of the Underworld

Ninth day, third month, year one

He's at it again! He only took one day of rest before He
started tinkering with His Creation, and He's been at
it non-stop since then. Now He's laying down the law,
harping on about Good and Evil, and planning a "Just say
no" campaign against my principal product lines—lust,
gluttony, greed, sloth, wrath, envy, and pride. Which,
incidentally, are some of my favorite hobbies, too. Why
can't He just leave well enough alone? How He expects
that young couple to be fruitful and multiply if they don't
get into all that stuff is beyond me. I'll have to have a quiet
word with them.

[a continuation of previous entry]

"Sins," Lord Killjoy calls them—I was hoping to market them as "recreational leisure-time pursuits," which has more of a ring to it, but I suppose we're stuck with His brand-name now, even though nothing's on tablets of stone yet. Coming up with that list of seven has stolen my thunder (I've been meaning to publish some promotional material and a set of guidelines, but it's been hellishly busy down here), but I'll be damned if I'll let Him have the last word. Shame that the best ones are all accounted for; perhaps I could come up with something new, a truly original sin....

Sins List

1. Lust. Responsible Demon: Asmodeus
2. Gluttony. RD: Beelzebub
3. Greed RD: Mammon
4. Sloth. RD: Belphegor
5. Wrath. RD: Gaap
6. Envy. RD: Leviathan
7. Pride. RD: Lucifer
8. ???? RD: Self?

The original snake in the grass

First day, sixth month, year one

It's high time we expanded our client base. At the moment there's just that couple in Eden, and that's not good for business. A loophole in the law has allowed me to extend my boundary into a corner of the garden, and the tree I planted there is fruiting nicely; "apples," I think I'll call them, or maybe "passion fruit." Their aphrodisiac properties have always worked for me, so it should be plain sailing from there on.

You show me yours . . .

For shame!

As easy as pie

Third day, ninth month, year seven

My apple ploy has had the desired result. Once Adam and
Eve found out what they'd been missing, they were at it
like rabbits. It's a drag she decided to put some clothes
on, but you can't have everything! She's had a couple of
sons already, and another on the way. Cain is shaping
up nicely—but Abel shows a worrying tendency to virtue.
Should I intervene? I mean, am I his brother's keeper?

Last day, last month, year 1655

The "original sin" idea seems to be paying off.
Population figures all over the Earth are booming.
These humans have really got the hang of lust and being
fruitful, as well as all the other sins, and it's paying
dividends down here. A gratifyingly large proportion of
them end up with me, and The Guy Upstairs is not at all
happy with the way things are going. Well, He's got only
Himself to blame—if He hadn't given me the push, things
could have been very different.

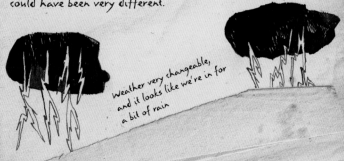

Weather very changeable,
and it looks like we're in for
a bit of rain

First day, third month, year 1665

What a hypocrite! Mr. "Wrath is a Sin" doesn't like the way things are going down on Earth, so He conjures up a deluge to wipe out all the wicked sinners. Double standards or what? My hard work will end up going down the drain.

There is a glimmer of hope though; old goody-two-shoes Noah has been given permission to build a boat for his family and breeding pairs of some of the more useful animals. Maybe one of his sons could be tempted to act as my inside man and perhaps smuggle a few verminous and disease-ridden stowaways on board, too.

NOTE TO SELF: get the R & D department to hurry up with the woodworm breeding program.

MOUNT ARARAT MARINA
PRICE LIST FOR MOORING:

Rafts, rowboats, and coracles.... **10 shekels/day**
Pleasure boats (up to 250 cubits).... **100 shekels/day**
Oceangoing vessels and arks (over 250 cubits).... **1000 talents/day**

Last day, eighth month, year 1665

Flood damage has severely interrupted operations in the netherworld and dampened our spirits. Communications have also been disrupted, just when we need them most—the deluge has resulted in a huge influx of lost souls and transporting them here is a real problem. All my good intentions have had to be put on hold, as the repaving of the road to Hell is our top priority.

My New Year Resolutions

1. *Be more tempting*
2. *Learn to love rats*
3. *Start smoking*
4. *Start drinking to excess*
5. *Invent packing peanuts*
6. *Make work for idle hands*
7. *Raise price of souls*
8. *Get out and meet more people*
9. *Make purgatory more boring*
10. *Develop reality game shows*
11. *Make 8th deadly sin*
12. *Kick ass*
13. *Copyright best tunes*

A lock from
my lovely

The future Mr. and Mrs. S?

Sixth day, sixth month, year 1701

I don't know what's come over me. I've always had
a healthy lust-life, and there's been a plentiful supply
of female company since the Fall. But this is different.
Lilith (oh, Lilith!) has been a faithful handmaiden
since the beginning, but it was only when she let her
hair down and took off the
spectacles that I noticed—she's
beautiful! I've never felt like
this about anybody, all soft
and sympathetic. Can this
be love?

What's a nice girl like you
doing in a place like this?

Seventh day, third month, year 1702

A real red-letter day—I'm a daddy! Eat
your hearts out Adam and Eve! Lilith's
given birth to twins, Incubus and Succubus.
Only a few hours old and they're already
little imps. I think young Inky takes after
his father (such cute little horns and
talons), but Sucka is the spitting (!) image
of her mom. It's such a relief to have
some heirs for the business, to carry on the bad work.
I never imagined myself as the paternal type, but now
I can see the benefits of a large family.

Twin evils: Sucka and Inky

What a comfort

[Undated]

Have just arrived for a visit to our offices in Babylon. My boys have established a real presence here, with agents working right across Mesopotamia [modern Iraq]. This is certainly where the action is these days, and I wonder if I shouldn't concentrate all my operations here for the time being. It's possibly an area ripe for long-term plans, too.

Also spent some time with the W of B*; these business trips can be so demanding, one has to have a little R & R. I'm glad all that lovey-dovey stuff with Lilith wore off. Must have been something I ate. (L must never get wind of this or she'll make life Hell for me.)

Babylon offers so many attractive possibilities!

[*The Whore of Babylon.]

[a continuation of previous entry]

It's gratifying to see what the Babylonians have achieved using the aid budget we've negotiated with them. The gardens are a delight, although there seems to have been some misunderstanding of the terms of the grant: as yet there have been no public hangings. Building work is well underway on the Tower of Babel, which should attract visitors to the city, and there's already a cosmopolitan feel to the place with workers from all over the world. I feel they really understand what I'm saying here.

PATENT CERTIFICATE FOR PLAGUES

1. Rivers and other water sources turned to blood ("Dam")
2. Reptiles (especially frogs) ("Tsfardeia")
3. Lice or gnats ("Kinim")
4. Flies and/or beetles ("Arov")
5. Pestilence, disease on livestock ("Dever")
6. Unhealable boils ("Shkhin")
7. Hail mixed with fire ("Barad")
8. Locusts ("Arbeh")
9. Darkness ("Choshech")
10. Death of the firstborn ("Makat Bechorot")

Awarded to Nicholas D. Satan

January 8, 1440 BC

A disturbing letter from Egypt. Pharaoh tells me Moses and Aaron have been stirring up discontent amongst the Hebrew slaves (who insist they're big G's "chosen few"—sounds like hubris to me). If that wasn't bad enough, they've asked for a bit of divine intervention and He's obliged with a series of plagues: blood in the water supply, frogs, lice, flies, anthrax, boils, hail and firebolts, locusts, blotting out the sun, and infant mortality—all MY ideas! If He wasn't omniscient, I'd suspect this was an inside job.

[a continuation of previous entry]

I've replied to Pharaoh, telling him to cut his losses rather than try to deal with the Hebrews. It's obvious G isn't going to play fair, so it's probably best in the long run to go down to Moses and let his people go. It should free up the Egyptians—who aren't a bad bunch and have a lot going for them. Anybody who worships jackals and promotes incest in the royal family can't be all bad.

I've sent him a small gift too, as a token of goodwill. A small poisonous serpent as a family pet. Might be useful one day.

May 1, 1350 BC

Here we go again. More laws being passed down from on high (I just knew that Moses was going to be trouble). Our legal department's working flat out just to keep up with all the new legislation. If there's going to be any kind of justice, we'll have to separate the executive from the judiciary—or at least make provision for a few by-laws and amendments. Let's see what we've got this time....

TEN ~~EVIL~~ COMMANDMENTS

1. ~~I am the Lord thy God.~~ Thou shalt have no other gods before me.

Mister High and Mighty's getting too damned righteous. Thou shalt prefer the Devil to Him.

TABLETS OF STONE— HOW PRETENTIOUS IS THAT?

2. Thou shalt ~~not make to thyself any~~ graven images.

Thou shalt feel free to portray me in all my glory (especially if thou captureth my rugged good looks, etc.).

3. Thou ~~shalt not take the name of the Lord~~ thy God in vain.

Thou shouldst blaspheme, cuss, and utter profanities whenever things don't go thy way.

4. ~~Remember the Sabbath day,~~ to keep it holy.

Thou shalt use the weekends profitably to catch up with all the sins thou hast missed out on during the week.

5. Honor thy ~~Father and thy Mother.~~

Ensure the life insurance and wills are up to date.

Cheap trick, that burning bush

6. ~~Thou shalt not kill.~~

Thou shalt not let any slight go unavenged.

7. Thou shalt ~~not~~ commit adultery.

Thou shalt not get found out.

And what was wrong with the golden calf?

8. ~~Thou shalt not~~ steal.

Thou shalt consider it an "indefinite loan."

9. ~~Thou shalt not bear false witness.~~

Thou shalt be economical with the truth.

10. Thou shalt ~~not~~ desire thy neighbor's wife, ~~neither shalt thou~~ covet thy neighbor's house, his field, or his manservant, or his maidservant, his ox, or his ass, or anything that is thy neighbor's.

Oh, come on! Thou shalt desire and covet to thy heart's content, especially if it's a nice ass.

March 6, 200 BC

The Romans have done very well for themselves (with a bit of assistance from our organization), snapping up franchise options all around the Mediterranean and into Europe, taking slaves, and spreading the cultural advantages of orgies and gladiatorial entertainment. Since vanquishing the Greeks, who were a tiresomely virtuous race, they've taken over some of their better ideas, including some of the more colorful gods. I've been particularly struck by the Furies—I wish I'd thought of them, as just at the moment Hell hath no Fury like those women, scorned though they might be. I've gained a foothold in the pantheon too, in the guise of Pan with a retinue of satyrs. The ladies like a toot on the pipes.

Horny little devil, aren't I?

December 25, 5 BC

Rumors are rife concerning the imminent coming of a Messiah; even the Romans and the Hebrews are getting worked up about it. One of my spies tells me that the Great Holy Roller is envious of my growing brood (I've been enjoying myself quite a bit, I must admit), and is now telling everyone He's planning a family too. How Mr. Homeboy thinks he'll do that when he hasn't even got a girlfriend, I don't know. Still, if it's true, I'll need a contingency plan; a representative on Earth to redress the balance. There are already a few (665, if memory serves me correctly) operating up there on a part-time basis and I've kept tabs on them, but one more, a sort of contra-Messiah (Antichrist?) wouldn't go amiss. Mustn't forget to mark him with the number, to avoid confusion.

BLAH, BLAH

BLAH, BLAH

BLAH, BLAH

Spread the word—the alternative lifestyle's on its way

March 25, 1 BC

I sent one of my boys up to Nazareth on a routine seduction mission, but he came back with his tail between his legs and a pathetic tale to tell. The girl he'd had his eye on, Mary, told him she'd just had a visit from that sycophantic facilitator Gabriel, who had given her some interesting news, and she was having quite enough trouble explaining things to her fiancé, and then having to go to the tax office in Bethlehem to register for family assistance, so really couldn't get involved. I don't know why I bother dealing with all this trivial incompetence.

MEMO TO BETHLEHEM TAX OFFICE
....
Please send details of any couple named Joseph and Mary from Nazareth. I believe they're attempting a welfare scam.

Volume II

Out With the Old, In With the New

....

New Testament, Revelations, and Apocrypha

➤➤➤

* The Nativity

* Birth of Christianity * The Romans

* Jesus gets a following

* Attempts at a merger: tempting terms

* Judas, a minor success

* The Crucifixion

* St. John's "revelations"

* The Four Horsemen and Armageddon

* Finding a way into the publishing monopoly of the gospels

"What do you mean, coming down here, blowing your trumpet, frightening the sheep, creating a nuisance.... We're quite happy abiding in our field if it's all the same to you. I already know what a baby looks like, now butt out...." Oh, if only those shepherds had read my script

Stirring up trouble with the agricultural workers

January 1, 1 AD

What a way to start the New Year. We've now got a Son of G to contend with, as well as all those angels and other assorted do-gooders. I didn't think He'd do it, given all His guidelines on non-mortal insemination and the Genetic Code. I know my boys have been at it for years, but that's not the point; He's supposed to be above all that. Think of the logistical practicalities of impregnating that girl.... On second thoughts, let's not go there. And the publicity He'll get. This could set my business back centuries.

January 6, 1 AD

Oh, very clever. He's made a media circus of this "Christmas" business, and it's so popular it could even become an annual event. First, He creates a big new star right over the stable they're using as a maternity unit, then He employs three media moguls from the East to oversee the publicity (wise guys, by all accounts). And now everybody's flocking to Bethlehem to see what all the fuss is about. Herod and the Romans are hopping mad, but I can't see a way of keeping the lid on this one, dammit.

PRESS RELEASE from G's Pub. Dept.—tacky, or what?

June 5, 1 AD

There's a distressing air of optimism in Judaea after J's arrival. In the Good vs. Evil struggle, as ever, the Devil takes the hindmost. I do my best from down here, but seem doomed to always be No. 2. It's so depressing to realize that He always has the edge, being omnipotent—why can't He fight fair? Whenever I start making some progress, getting in touch with my feelings and acting on my inner demons, I get summoned by some non-entity and can't achieve closure. Maybe I'll get a break some time ... but until then, sufficient unto the day (whatever the Hell that means).

Virgil P. Olympus, LCSW
COUNSELING AND THERAPY

Your next appointment is: *10 am, June 6* at the Wellbeing Center, Jericho

Do you need help to give up smoking?
Ask for our information pack at Reception

"The Age of Innocents"
downtown Bethlehem, Winter 1 AD

December 28, 1 AD

Meeting with Herod. He's not at all happy, even though our agreement gave him a nice little arrangement with the Romans, the kingdom of Judaea, and ten wives. What more does he want? But now he storms back, moaning that he isn't the Messiah too—well, he should have read the small print. Massacring the children of Bethlehem, laudable though it is, won't change things either: payback time is looming. A deal's a deal, Mr. Herod.

June 6, 6 AD

I mustn't let all this business in the Middle East distract me. The new kid got some media attention and now has a bit of a following, but so what? I've got friends too—in fact, I've got pretty good popularity ratings with Barbarians worldwide. Long-term plans involve Huns and Mongol hordes, but for the moment I'll concentrate on mobilizing the Goths. I like their style—it might even catch on as some kind of youth movement some day—but they still lack organization.

Great outfit—smart, but practical

The sort of fashion statement I'm comfortable with

A good ceremony with all the trimmings would add gravitas

July 4, 17 AD

It's all very well being the head of a successful multinational operation, and I must admit I enjoy striking terror now and then, but it would be nice to be revered too, or at least shown a bit of respect. I mean, these humans have worshiped some pretty strange things—especially the Egyptians (a dung beetle? Even I draw the line somewhere). J's got himself a cozy little entourage of devotees and even his mom has admirers. I wonder if I could have a religion of my own? Luciferism or something? Devilism? Satanianity? Eviltude??

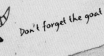

Don't forget the goat

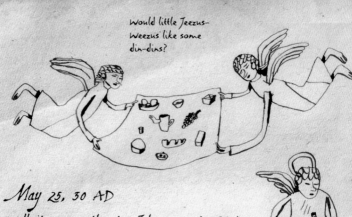

Would little Jeezus-
Weezus like some
din-dins?

May 25, 30 AD

Well, it was worth a try. J has gone AWOL in
the desert without food and water. I suppose
he's trying to "find himself" or something.
I don't know where young people get these
ideas. I thought I'd take the opportunity
to have a quiet chat with him, see if he
could be persuaded to see things from my
perspective. It didn't go well, though; he's a
stubborn young man. If I'm honest (which isn't often), I lost
my cool and the discussion degenerated into name-calling.
To my shame, I ended up taunting him with "If you're so
wonderful, why don't you turn the stones into bread, jump
off this pinnacle etc.," but he wasn't having any of it. I tried
to regain some dignity by storming off with
"Your loss, not mine," but the effect was
spoiled by the arrival of a band of grinning
angels with a picnic for him.

IN THE FUTURE, I'LL APPOINT A DEVIL'S
ADVOCATE FOR THIS SORT OF JOB.

My new pet; at least
my trip to the desert
wasn't a complete
waste of time

May 26, 30 AD

I must try to be positive, especially after yesterday's debacle. It was nice to get out a bit and enjoy some of my contributions to the Creation. Deserts are such wonderfully inhospitable places, quite like home. If I could introduce some unsustainable agricultural practices, perhaps we could have a few more of them.

Prototype "Dust Bowl" suitable for all continents

With luck, nobody will notice the horns . . .

. . . but with those short skirts, the tails might arouse suspicion

September 14, 30 AD

A breakthrough. It's always been difficult getting in on the Roman market, as they seem to be capable of all sorts of excesses without any help from me, but a couple of my boys have managed to infiltrate the Praetorian Guard and stir things up. Once the emperor, Tiberius, was aware of the personal benefits my involvement could offer, there was no stopping him. The contract was signed today, officially sanctioning the appointment of my agents—effectively a friendly takeover of their operations in Europe and Asia Minor. BOOYEAH!

In vino veritas

March 15, 31 AD

To Rome again for further negotiations
with Tiberius. Not that he's trying to wriggle out of his
contractual obligations—far from it. He wants to extend
the franchise to the rest of his dynasty (he introduced
me to his nephew Caligula, a delightfully spoiled brat)
with options for a hereditary renewal clause. With such
a dysfunctional family, things can only get better. In the
meantime, I've given him free reign to enjoy himself with
orgies and slaughter, beer and circuses, or whatever takes
his fancy. Most satisfactory.

Invitation

Invitatus es Ad orgiae et caudae pullo-
rum preprandiae, in Palatio Imperatorio
VII horae, Ides Martis

A night to remember,
so they tell me

TONIGHT
ON THE MOUNT
Open-air performance by
Jesus of Nazareth.
THE ACT THE AUTHORITIES
WOULD LIKE TO BAN.
ENTRANCE FREE, BUT SPACE LIMITED, SO GET THERE EARLY!
ONE NIGHT ONLY!

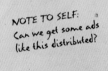

NOTE TO SELF:
Can we get some ads like this distributed?

April 2, 31 AD

J is such an angry young man. It's a shame he couldn't be tempted to work for me. But now he's on a mission to change the world (fat chance), and has been drawing crowds all over the place with his one-man roadshow. Pretty puerile stuff—a bit of healing, some minor miracles, and way too much sermonizing, but the audiences lap it up and—don't ask me why—the women love him. It'll all end in tears.

If he carries on upsetting the powers that be, he'll come to a sticky end—they don't like being upstaged.

Heads I win, tails you lose

May 2, 31 AD

Who the Hell does He think He is?
I set up some clients with a currency
exchange and livestock business in
the temple in Jerusalem, and while
they're carrying out their legitimate trade
in the temple, in sweeps Mr. Spoilsport and knocks
down all their stalls. Sometimes he really goes too far.
And don't give me any of that "Render unto Caesar..."
crap. Messing about with independent bankers like that
could seriously destabilize the economy, with disastrous
results for my business operations. I ought to have him
arrested. In fact, I think I will!

The root of all evil—so don't
mess with it

April 10, 32 AD

J is planning a night out in a restaurant with his coterie of yes-men. It's supposed to be some kind of reward for their loyalty, but if past experience is anything to go by, they'll be lucky to get anything more than bread and wine. Why do they stick with him? Don't they realize that, thanks to his subversive activities, this could be the last supper they'll get out of him? I could use an inside man now: that Thomas looks a bit doubtful and I've got some dirt on Judas, so could try leaning on him a little....

MEMO TO CHIEF OF POLICE, 9TH PRECINCT, JERUSALEM
....
Could you pop into my office sometime today? I have some information that may be to our mutual benefit, concerning a certain political troublemaker. I am sure I can count on you to take the necessary action....

The condemned man ate a hearty meal (NOT!!)

April 11, 33 AD

All set up for tonight's dinner. The authorities have been notified, so it's showtime. It was woefully simple to get Judas on our side (30 pieces of silver? Pitiful!), but the others were so holier-than-thou. Some of these so-called Apostles have even started writing their memoirs and biographies of their darling leader in a bid to make publishing history. Oh, I'm sure they'll sell a few copies and even the picture rights for the meeting tonight, but it's a bit of a one-shot deal compared to what I've achieved over the millennia.

NOTE TO SELF: Perhaps I should prepare MY journals for publication sometime?

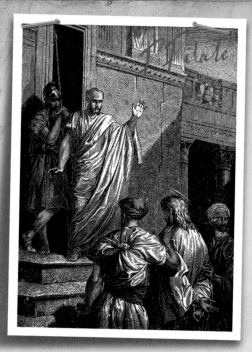

From a grateful P.P. Could be the making of him!

April 12, 33 AD

Everything went according to plan. A police raid on downtown Jerusalem, rounding up all the usual suspects and J arrested on suspicion of treasonous activism. Yes! Judas really delivered the goods at the ID parade and his evidence was the kiss of death to Big G's boy and his interference. I've booked my seat for the trial (tickets are already selling fast), which should be highly entertaining.

April 13, 33 AD

You've got to hand it to that Pontius Pilate, he really knows how to work a crowd. I just hope he remembers who taught him so well. And where did he find that Barabbas? A masterstroke. J didn't come over well in the cross-examination (but then, he had been roughed up a bit in the cells), and the mob ended up baying for his blood. Pilate passed sentence with an easy conscience and I can now wash my hands of the whole business.

April 14, 33 AD

J (and, unfortunately, a couple of my business associates—collateral damage, I suppose. Never mind, I can write it off) was taken up to Calvary for crucifixion this morning. That's the last we'll hear of him—if there's any justice! It means I can relax over the weekend—in fact, I'm thinking of extending it and suggest making Monday a public holiday.

A well-earned rest

Shopping list —

RABBIT

EGGS

CHOCOLATE

A tad over the top for a business card, don't you think, Nero?

December 25, 67 AD

Young Nero (a nice lad, fond of music, but with a fiery temper) sent me an advance copy of the latest sci-fi blockbuster, *Apocalypse* by "Saint" John. "A revelation," it says in the blurb, and it's certainly better than all the pious ramblings you normally get from that school of writers, but a best-seller? I don't think so. He paints a reassuring picture of Armageddon, but spoils it with all the numerology, angels, trumpets, and stuff, and then loses the plot completely when he goes on about salvation. What was he on? Jimson weed?

January 1, 68 AD

Reading that *Apocalypse* has got me thinking. When it comes to the crunch, are my troops ready for the big push? I'm tending to rely on the cavalry division, or at least the Four Horsemen leading them, but how reliable are they? Truth is, they're all loose cannons and although they can work well together, it's difficult to get them to sit down and work out a strategy. Should I spearhead the campaign with Famine or Pestilence? Or maybe send in War right from the start? Whatever, I'll need Death as backup—but he always seems so busy… At this rate the final showdown won't get underway until the Millennium.

Our brave boys at the Front

Trouble is, I can never remember which one's which

Too hot to handle? Me?

October 3, 75 AD

Since having the kids Lilith's not the woman she used to be in the bedroom department. Anyway, most nights she seems to be out with the other old bats. So I can hardly be blamed for seeking my creature comforts elsewhere. Even chief executives have needs. In any case, I had business down in Mesopotamia and it would have been churlish not to look up the old Whore of B, who certainly scrubs up well still. I wonder what her secret is? This really is a great place. I can imagine coming back here time and time again over the years. The slightest pretext and bang, back here I'll be. I could make it my own Hell on Earth....

The spark's still there

when in Rome, wear a condom

November 20, 289 AD

Well, who'd have thought it—Son of G has actually pulled
it off. The stunt of a comeback appearance after the
crucifixion got quite a cult following, but I never thought
it would catch on like this. It's disheartening, the way they
go around stirring up peace and goodwill all over the place.
Even the Romans have fallen for it and are giving up their
old gods in favor of Christianism or whatever they call it.
It's not all bad news though: we were getting damned busy
and overcrowded down here, so it was a relief when Neptune,
Bacchus, Venus, and Pluto (or Dis, as he insists on being
called these days, even though I thought of the name first)
came over to our side, and we could colonize the Roman
and Greek Underworld as it fell into disuse. Dis use! I like
it—very droll.

February 23, 291 AD

If I'm going to prevail in this battle against insidious Good, I've got to win the propaganda war first. It's galling that the evangelical set beat me to it with their scriptures (and those tedious letters Paul banged off to everybody he could think of), but surely nobody takes their word as gospel? I've put the Communications Department on the case. They've already come up with an impressive set of forged documents (though I'm not sure that *Apocrypha* is a good code name) subtly raising doubts on the official line. Unfortunately a set of scrolls smearing the opposition has gone missing: apparently the author got drunk celebrating his success at one of the Dead Sea resorts. Heads will roll.

and lo, it came to pass that the son of G
with women of low character: and he saith
unto them that believeth that will believe anythin
and embrace the Devil and all his works
as I say, not as I do. And amass the riches
sucker an even break. Thus shall ye achieve

Volume III

The Good Old Days

(The Dark Ages)

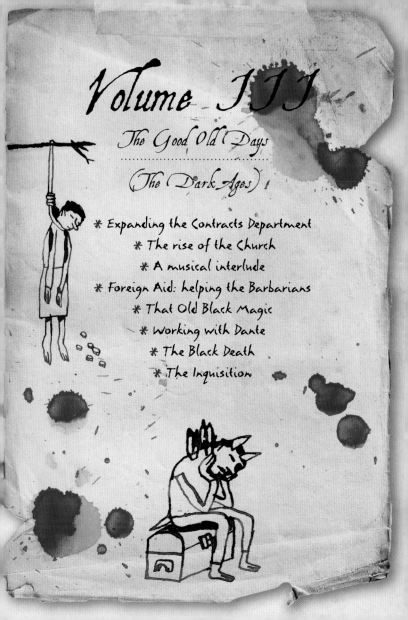

September 25, 295

Things are quieter with the mortals these days, apart from a few outbreaks of virtue and morality, and I've arranged with Diocletian* for these to be dealt with severely. In fact, I've got so many people on the payroll up there now, it's given me a chance to concentrate on some administrative reforms down here. The Contracts Department is overloaded and understaffed (a victim of its own success), and I think Big G has picked up quite a few repentant souls when we haven't been on top of the paperwork. This just won't do.

Emperor D with the draft of his first Edict Against the Christians (ghostwritten by guess who)

[* Gaius Aurelius Valerius Diocletianus, ruthless and virulently anti-Christian Emperor of Rome 284–305.]

October 1, 295

A useful meeting with the heads of Administration, Contracts, and Human Resources (the new name for the Client Management department). Thanks to a recruiting drive amongst the middle classes we have an army of literate guests with us now—and what could be a better repayment for their Earthly indulgences than an eternity of secretarial work? They should be able to keep tabs on who owes us what. I've also approved the new all-purpose contract*, drawn up by that rogue Nero (who's settled here nicely and is anxious to please), and set up a team of scribes making copies for future use. Better than jotting things on a scrap of parchment every time I'm summoned.

[* See attached sample contract inside front cover.]

Give 'em the old
Hun two!

June 11, 434

Something of a coup today: received a summons from
Attila, who's just been made joint Khan of the Huns
(with his brother, a real wimp) and is looking for some
advice on empire-building. This puts me in an awkward
position vis à vis the Romans, but after a bit of horse
trading, I persuaded him to concentrate his sacking and
pillaging on the Persians for the time being. All the same,
his enthusiasm for slaughter could come in useful if the
Roman Empire continues going soft, and it would be nice
to see a bit more action in Europe again. I like Attila—
he's clever as well as ruthless, and can appreciate the
power of unscrupulous diplomacy as well as terror.
He should go far.

Just love
those horns....

FIND OUT WHO'S
WORKING FOR US IN
CENTRAL EUROPE THESE
DAYS. I LOSE TRACK! IT'S
BEST IF WE CAN GET
THEM ALL SINGING FROM
THE SAME HYMNAL
(SO TO SPEAK).

A the H at the equestrian
sports meeting

October 6, 452

On my advice, Attila has removed the inconvenience of
joint rule with his brother (who arrived with us a short
while ago), and taken the opportunity to expand his good
works into Roman territory. You have to admire his nerve.
He's done deals with just about everybody—Goths, Vandals,
Gauls, and even the Romans—and then stabbed them in the
back with a Hunnish invasion. It's about time Rome got
a bloody nose, what with their craven submission to that
pontificating "Papa" Leo and his Catholics. Attaboy, Attila!

Why can't I have Earthly offices like this?

January 1, 500

Five hundred years since that upstart J appeared on the scene, and he's still a thorn in my side!* More than ever, actually, despite the efforts of many of my best clients. People are so easily swayed by fashion, which at the moment is dominated by what they're doing in Italy (though I'll grudgingly admit that those Italians have got style). The head office of the Church in Rome is opening branches throughout Europe and the Middle East, and controls most of the media, making life very difficult. I think it's time we infiltrated the House of G before things get out of hand.

[* Satan is being uncharacteristically ironic here. He quotes from II Corinthians 12:7, "There was given to me a thorn in the flesh, the messenger of Satan to buffet me."]

September 3, 590

Finding a way in to the Church was easier than I thought.
The ridiculous rule of celibacy in the monasteries and
convents (even I couldn't have come up with an idea as
unmerciful as that) left the door wide open for temptation.
You'd be amazed how many monks and nuns have signed
up for the chance of an illicit liaison or two. In return,
they've set up all manner of heretical organizations, which
should keep their new boss Gregory busy for a while—he
soon won't have much to chant about! Which reminds me:
some of my latest monastic recruits are really into music,
but found the psalm-
singing scene less than
funky (Papa G's the
guy who put the
"plain" in plainsong),
so they're busy spicing
up the repertoire.*
Not exactly hot stuff
yet, but with them
and the troubadours
I should get all the
best tunes.

Altogether now . . .

[* The dissonant sound of the augmented fourth or tritone, much used in jazz,
appeared only occasionally in medieval music: known as the *diabolus in musica*,
it was proscribed by the Church.]

THE CORONATION OF CHARLEMAGNE
IMPERATOR AUGUSTUS
OF THE HOLY ROMAN EMPIRE
conducted by Pope Leo III

Adulterer, perjurer, and all-round good guy

PROGRAMME OF EVENTS:

10 a.m.: Procession to the Basilica

11 a.m.: Thanksgiving Service 2 hours!

1 p.m.: Formal Coronation Ceremony

3 p.m.: Mass (led by Pope Leo and the Cardinals)

7.30 p.m.: Acceptance Speech by Charlemagne

11 p.m.: Torchlit Procession and Close of Proceedings

And the party is where? Boring, boring, boring

December 25, 800

What's happened to Rome? I can't get over how much it has changed. It used to be such a fun city, and I could always rely on a friendly welcome. These days it's hard to find any decent (or indecent) nightlife, and orgies and circuses are a thing of the past—everybody's off to church all the time. Mass hysteria, I call it. I came up here for the coronation of Charlemagne, in the hope of catching up with some old friends at the celebrations, but it was an unbelievably dull affair, even with all the hype over Christmas. And now the town's run by those sanctimonious guys in dresses, we're told we've got to call it the Holy Roman Empire, would you believe? What is the world coming to?

May 19, 942

Christianity has spread like the plague (N.B. we haven't seen a good plague since the early days back in Egypt, must do something about this), and as if that wasn't troubling enough, some of my closest allies in the East have been sweet-talked by someone calling himself Muhammad. It's all very depressing. I'm on a sales trip in Northern Europe, and here in Britain the problem is just as bad. Doing door-to-door work in Glastonbury, I visited the local blacksmith, Dunstan,* for a pedicure. Normally they're only too happy to do business with me and positively relish the thought of an eternity of forge work—but this one turned out to be a real Bible-thumper. He quite put my nose out of joint.

Cold and wet—
nothing much seems
to happen round here.

Satan

[* St. Dunstan (909–988), who, legend has it, nailed a horseshoe to the Devil's hoof and grabbed him by the nose with a pair of red-hot tongs. This entry may be the source of the myth.]

february 7, 1206

At last, a light at the end of the tunnel. The last couple of centuries, I've almost felt like calling it quits, but today I had a call that has bucked me up. Until now, I haven't had much to do with the Asian market (my agent Yama* effectively has the franchise), so I was pleased to hear from Mongolia—Genghis, the latest in the Khan dynasty, is looking for investors for his empire-building. His business plan is sound and could be just what I'm looking for: he's already got the manpower by bringing the various Mongol hordes together, and is confident that with the right backing he can take all of Asia by storm. Why stop there? I asked him—now the Huns have lost their nerve, the market in Europe is wide open too.

[*Yama: the Lord of Death in Indian, Chinese, and Japanese mythology.]

August 9, 1279

The Khan family have done extremely well for themselves, once they'd accepted the terms of my stake in their success. They've shown continuous growth for over three-quarters of a century, and the latest figures to come in show a 30 percent share of the market. We—sorry, they—are on the brink of a breakthrough into Europe, so long as they can maintain their aggressive sales techniques. Our only fear is the current Khan, Kublai. He lacks the tenacity and vision of his grandfather: he seems to have no interest in rape or pillage, and just dreams of pleasure domes in Xanadu.

WITCHES—BOON OR CURSE?

Stirring up trouble

A burning issue

October 31, 1300

I suppose I should be pleased with the way Black Magic has caught on recently. Flattered even, with the rise of Satanism. Well, I don't want to seem ungrateful—and I know a lot of Dark Arts practitioners sincerely believe they're doing some good—but I wish they'd consulted me first. It was my idea, after all, although I never had the time to organize it properly. I blame the Pagans. Once they got it into their heads that they were an oppressed minority and set up Witchcraft protest groups, the whole anti-establishment movement got quite trendy and all sorts of woolly-minded "free thinkers" jumped on the bandwagon. The whole thing's going off at half cock now and runs the risk of becoming respectable.

[a continuation of previous entry]

What gets my goat is the hypocrisy (not that I disapprove of hypocrisy per se, but this is galling). Most of these "Devil worshipers" lead disgracefully decent lives and salve their consciences by observing a Black Sabbath a couple of times a year. There's no commitment to the core values, just a routine adherence to the rituals. And where did they get all that stuff about black chickens and virgins from? Apart from the sacrificial element, the Black Mass is an insult—a sacrilegious travesty of what I had in mind. As for the witches' fixation with broomsticks, cats, and herbs, it's just too homely for words. I've got contacts in the Church; I'll get them to persecute a few more heretics as an example.

Thanks for a most
illuminating visit

Dante Alighieri
Poet and Travel Writer
Strada da Rovinare 1
Firenze
Italia

Remember to take this guy
off the mailing list

March 3, 1307

I seem to be going round and round in circles these days. Spent most of today with that infernal idiot Dante Alighieri explaining how the system works, and even arranging a guided tour with my man Virgil, but am beginning to regret the contract with him. Apart from painting a rather lurid picture of my operations, he treats the whole thing as something of a joke, and refers to my surroundings as "simply divine"—tact is obviously not his strong point. Still, I must not abandon all hope yet.

September 15, 1321

I wish I'd never done that deal with Dante. Since his death, he's done nothing but moan about conditions down here—and he does go on so. What did he expect? He should have known that visiting a place and having a good time is one thing, but it's a different matter when you have to live there. It came as a shock to him when he realized where he'd ended up; he didn't think I was serious. Well, surprise, surprise Mr. D! How else did you think you'd get all the info you needed to complete that tedious poem of yours?

It's not like he didn't know what he was letting himself in for

We've heard it all before Dante—many, many times

Need to keep track of satisfied customers

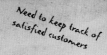

January 1, 1347

New Year's resolution: to make my presence felt more. It's about time I manifested myself on a larger scale. It's all very well picking up the odd soul and provoking discontent here and there, but I miss the old days of plague and pestilence. The wonks down in Biological Research have been breeding a new species of rat that might just do the trick: tests on some of our long-term guests have brought on reassuringly unpleasant symptoms, and they're ready for field trials. All it needs now is a snappy slogan...
something like "The Black Nasty" or "The Dreadful Death"? I'll work on it.

Any chance of prolonging an agonizing death?

Could have spin-off in the fashion trade

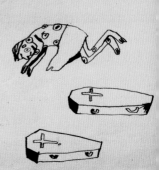

February 10, 1347

All's well that ends well. There was a minor panic in the labs last week when a pair of the best breeders went missing. The research geeks had hushed it all up, and the first I knew about it was this afternoon—I suspect they weren't going to tell me either, but they've got away with it this time. Bubo and Pandemica (the little rascals that escaped) were spotted in Turkey, with a healthy litter of children, making their way west. Early reports suggest the pestilence they're carrying is catching on faster than expected, and long-term forecasts are healthy—or rather, unhealthy—with outbreaks likely in all areas well into the 17th century.

Go forth and multiply, my little ones!

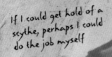

If I could get hold of a scythe, perhaps I could do the job myself

June 29, 1351

A bit of pestilence never goes amiss, especially with such satisfyingly gruesome symptoms, but it means I have to work closely with Death, coordinating the migration of souls so that our workforce can deal with the rush of new arrivals. Perhaps I'm being overly suspicious, but I don't know if he can be trusted. Big G uses him too, although not on the same scale, and I'm not sure where his loyalties lie. It's risky employing freelancers like him, but you just can't get the staff these days.

July 4, 1351

I need a holiday. The plagues have upped my workload
to a ridiculous level and the strain is beginning to show.
Success isn't all it's cracked up to be—I'm continually
having to watch my back as I'm sure my achievements
have caused some jealousy. Or am I being paranoid?
Take this afternoon: interminable meetings, first with
Death, then Old Father Time, both wrangling for a slice
of the action. Is it just me, or are they uncannily similar?
Has anybody ever seen them in the same room together?

Death and
Father
Time—spot
the difference

December 2, 1456

Vlad III of Wallachia

Dear Satan

Your assistance recently has been invaluable. I'm now back in business, and making the point felt in no uncertain terms! And it's all thanks to your inspiration and guidance — I would never have thought of the imp

So cheering to get a proper letter, something you can really get your teeth into

December 9, 1456

A nice letter this morning from Vlad Dracula, thanking me for my help in regaining his throne in Romania. It's nice to get such an appreciative client, particularly one with such a penetrating insight into my modus operandi. He's had bad press recently, often accused of being beyond the pale, but although he can be a bit bloodthirsty, his heart's in the right place. I'm gratified to hear that he's still eager to fulfill his side of our bargain, considering he has so much at stake.

[a continuation of previous entry]

I've been thinking about how well Vlad has done. What's the secret of his success? His ruthlessness, of course, but most of all his talent for propaganda—he has encouraged rumors that he is a vampire, which of course he's not. Yet. But he would be good at the job, a sort of figurehead for all the undead wandering the Earth at the moment. The Black Death has put such a strain on accommodations down here, I've had to put an increasing number of inmates to work elsewhere. For some reason, most of them end up in the Balkans, but perhaps now's the time to find alternative regions where they'll be more appreciated—Africa would be good, or the Caribbean (I've always liked Haiti). The Church has no influence there, and even denies its existence.

IDEAS FOR THE AFRO-CARIBBEAN MARKET

Alternative medicine? Witch doctor?

Zombie & Son

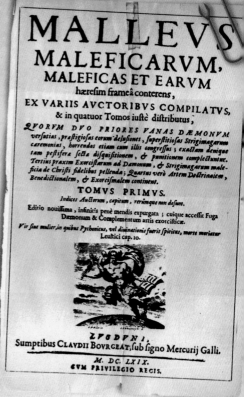

May 9, 1487

Life's so complicated these days. It's really messing with my mind. I get a few covens and Dark Arts groups going, then suddenly everybody's dabbling in it without the proper authority. People practicing as witches and Black Magicians without any training. So, I have a crackdown, using double agents in the Church to root out the worst offenders and make an example of them. What happens? They get over enthusiastic and the whole persecution thing gets out

[a continuation of previous entry]

of hand. Now the Pope's got involved and his boys are taking over punishment of heretics, with some of my loyal supporters caught in the cross-fire. The press is useless as well. I set it up to promote my brand and what do we get? Endless copies of the Bible—and some damn silly treatise on how to recognize and deal with witches, called *Malleus Maleficarum*. It's getting so you don't know who to trust.

The trouble with the press is that it's got into the wrong hands. While it's dominated by some Italian megalomaniac there's no chance of any balanced reporting, and we'll get more papal bull and nonsense like that *Malleus Maleficarum*. And what's with all the Latin still? Get with it—we're nearly in the 16th century, for Pete's sake! I need to look at ways of influencing the media up there in the future... some sort of international news corporation with somebody from down under controling channels of communication.*

DICTIONARY

Printer's devil:
noun A printers devil was an apprentice in a printing firm who would perform tasks such as mixing tubs of ink and fetching type. Several renowned men served as printer's devils in their youth

All very well, but what about getting a Devil's printer?

[* An idea that was eventually achieved some 500 years later, with a global communications empire owned by a single (interestingly, Australian) media mogul.]

August 3, 1492

You win some, you lose some. My advisers thought it would be a good idea for me to spend some time in Iberia, which is where the action is these days. Unfortunately I arrived too late to prevent Columbus setting off westwards with missionary zeal. (How did he get that idea? Has he been talking to young Copernicus? I told him to keep things quiet until we'd finished the charts.) Let's just hope he doesn't stumble across the Americas, or there'll be Hell to pay. On the plus side, however, I've got the Borgias looking after things in Italy, and the Inquisition is working nicely here in Spain, thanks to my old friend Torquemada.

[a continuation of previous entry]

The Spanish Inquisition has been a surprise hit, and should really go the distance. The idea's nothing new—I set the ball rolling back in the 1180s—but this production has got real panache. And the best bit is, I'm virtually running the show. Having an ally like Torquemada as Grand Inquisitor has made all the difference, as he's not too squeamish about using some of the techniques I developed in Purgatory, and now they've got the hang of some of the more complicated instruments of torture, I think I can leave them to their own devices.

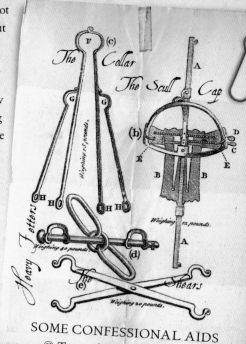

SOME CONFESSIONAL AIDS
© Tomas de Torquemada, 1492

August 15, 1504

Received an invitation from Hieronymous Bosch to a private view of his latest paintings. What an artist! If they're anything like the earlier ones, I'm in for a treat. Nobody else seems to have captured the beauty of my works so well. Is it really 50 years since he called on me for inspiration? I almost feel sorry for the sacrifice he has made for his art—but look forward to his company down here soon.

Invitation

You are invited to a private view of Earthly Delights and Purgatorial Punishments, an exhibition of the most recent oil paintings and drawings of Hieronymous Bosch, at The Gallery, Antwerp, 22 August at 7 pm

Volume IV

A Little Knowledge

(Renaissance and Enlightenment)

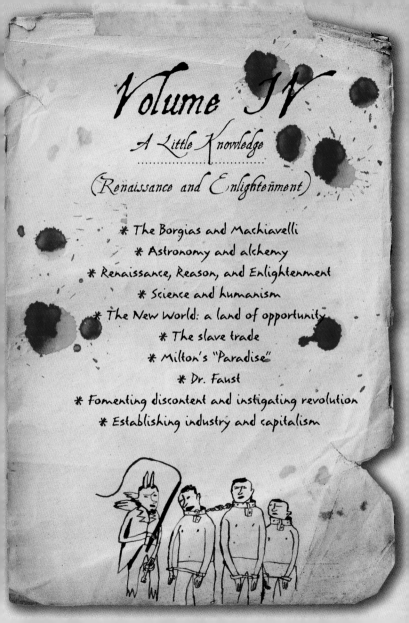

November 1, 1504

Hellfire and damnation! After all I've done for the Borgia family, that idiot Cesare lets me down by getting arrested. He could have been Pope, like his father and his grandfather before him—we had a good thing going there. It took a bit of doing too, rigging those elections. But oh no, Mr. Clever has to throw it all away for a career in politics. And now he's let them sneak a goody-goody back into the papacy I've lost control of the Church. Thanks a bundle, Cesare. At least we can still rely on your sister Lucrezia to keep her side of the bargain by marrying, seducing, or murdering whenever it's needed. Shame she can't be Pope.

LUCREZIA BORGIA TO WED AGAIN

Lucrezia Borgia, sister of disgraced Duke Cesare and daughter of the late Pope Alexander VI, is to marry for the third time, following the mysterious death of her second husband, Alfonso of Aragon. Amid rumors of murder, incest, and political intrigue, the bride-to-be was unconcerned by her brother's recent arrest as she

Calif...
Comm...
tions of...
est-ran...
cials...
started...
The...
mally...
cian into...
lo's offi...
Delg...
ing D...
ers a...
as "T...
the...
dress...

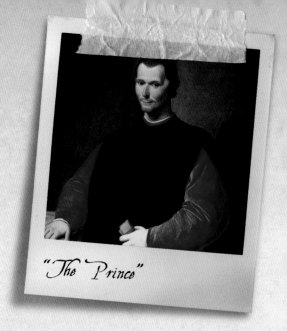

"The Prince"

May 3, 1508

Perhaps I was a little harsh on Cesare B. Since his arrival
down here, I realize he has a heart of gold ... and a brain
of horse manure. Great at cruelly wielding power, but
when it came to politics, he just wasn't up to the job.
If only that friend of his, Machiavelli, had come to me
earlier! Now there's a fella who really understands modern
diplomacy—it's all very well being ruthless, but these
days you have to be subtle too. It's too late for him to bring
the Church back into line, unfortunately, but we have to
think of the future: I'll suggest he write his ideas down
as a sort of handbook for any of my clients interested in
Government and the Civil Service.

Abandon hope all ye who enter here

Open 9 TO 5
After hours
service
available at
door marked
"LIMBO"

October 31, 1517

No sense of humor, some people. I thought the Germans might see the funny side of being part of the Holy Roman Empire, now that it's not holy, nor Roman, nor even an empire, but all my attempts to stir up a bit of healthy rebellion have been taken far too seriously. Instead of hitting the streets with a rebellion or two, or a bit of creative corruption—having some fun, in other words— they get some humorless do-gooder called Martin Luther to nail a list of complaints on his church door. 95 of them already! I tell you. Calls himself a Protestant, but he won't get any kind of reformation like that. They should take a leaf out of England's book. Their King Henry VIII takes no nonsense from Rome, and if anybody gets in the way of him having a good time, heads will roll.

December 14, 1555

Oh dear, oh dear. There's always one, isn't there? I
seem to get summoned by more than my fair share of
head-cases. This time it's an apothecary from France,
who seemed quite plausible when he first approached
me, but I realized too late that he'd probably been
sampling some of his own potions or something. This
Nostradamus (I should have known; what kind of a
name is that?) signed up to get some help publishing
his almanacs. Now I can't get rid of the guy. He comes
up with a different idea every week, and then—get this—
writes them in the form
of prophesies in execrably
impenetrable verse,
which he sends to me for
approval. I'm taking the
easy way out and just
humoring him. I predict
he'll soon be forgotten.

I see a bright
future for myself

NOSTRADAMUS

primaterial dragon

AN ALCHEMICAL MISCELLANY

green lion that swallows sun

androgynous spectral Antichrist

pot of melted gold

bird of Hermes

September 24, 1563

Encouraging signs of profanity in the academic world: the universities are getting fed up with toeing the ecclesiastical line, and scholars are looking for more "scientific" explanations. Fine by me, so long as they don't go too far—that's why I've introduced a few red herrings into the curriculum. Astrology's been popular for ages but, since the Church found out I was behind it, is now officially frowned upon. That should keep it on the syllabus! And despite the Creationists' bleating, I've managed (with help from Paracelsus) to get Alchemy into all the major faculties of chemistry, physics, and medicine. My ideas are enjoying quite a renaissance, and, if I can get the philosophers to see reason, may even lead to some kind of enlightenment.

October 5
[or 15*], 1582

It's sometimes the little
things that give me the
greatest pleasure. Pope
Gregory XIII has
been persuaded by
his astronomers to
adopt a new calendar
(I wonder who gave
them that idea? Tee
hee!), and today's
changeover day. Ten
days have gone missing. Mayhem
of course, especially as it's only in Italy, Spain, and
Portugal—the French say they'll get round to it soon, but
the Protestant countries won't have anything to do with
a Gregorian calendar. So nobody knows what day it is.
And all because I threw a wrench in the works during the
Creation, causing leap years and other anomalies that they
still haven't sorted out. Even the new system has the same
annoyingly different-length months. How about that for
forward planning?

OCTOBER 1582

6 Monday
7 Tuesday
8 Wednesday
9 Thursday
10 Friday
11 Saturday
12 Sunday
13 Monday
14 Tuesday
15 Wednesday
16 Friday

[* The dates in these journals use the Julian calendar up to this entry, and the
Gregorian thereafter.]

February 26, 1604

Here we go again. "Doctor" Faust (just how did he get that title?) sold his story to the press a few years ago, in breach of our agreement I might add, and now it's getting the literary treatment. Why is it attracting so much attention? He wasn't even a very good alchemist—too busy chasing skirt—and tried to worm his way out of his obligations when it came to the crunch. The latest in a line of "authorized biographies" comes from Christopher Marlowe, who really should know better, having bought my "How to achieve success as a writer" kit. I'm a bit hurt too. Who was it who covered for him when he got arrested for heresy and espionage? And then got him the job ghostwriting for that illiterate idiot Shakespeare? No gratitude, some people.

Will and Kit—spot the difference

The lesser of two evils

August 18, 1634

What an awkward position to be in: two of my clients facing each other in court. Of course, I'm going to have to let Cardinal Richelieu win the case, but not without some misgivings. He's already tortured his opponent, the priest Urbain Grandier, who unfortunately confessed to seducing the entire convent at Loudon* (although he says they were asking for it), and I can't prevent a public burning now. An unsatisfactory result, I'm afraid, as Richelieu is a difficult customer, and Grandier was doing such good work—but he did rather overstep the mark, poor devil.

[* The story of "The Devils of Loudon" was later sympathetically recounted by Aldous Huxley, and filmed by Ken Russell. UG was right, they were asking for it.]

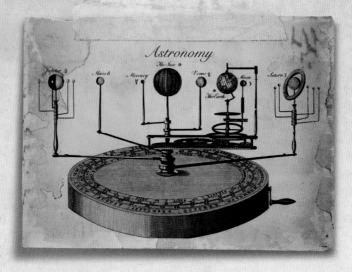

February 11, 1650

How times change. Only a millennium or so ago,
Christianity was the latest fad, now everybody's going
mad for science. Suits me. If they've got nothing better
to do with their time—and with the standard of living
improving like it is, they don't have anything better to do—
it sure beats going to church. I must admit I've encouraged
it (making work for idle hands and all that). I showed
Galileo a trick or two, regrettably landing him in hot water
but getting a good bit of media attention, and more recently
persuaded René Descartes to ask a few awkward questions
too. With a bit of luck (and a little more help from yours
truly) this should undermine the power of the Church.

[a continuation of previous entry]

Hang on a minute—let's think this through. It's all very well having the intellectuals question the authority of the Church, but whose side are they really on? All this scientific knowledge and "Age of Reason" nonsense could get out of hand if I'm not careful. Before you know it, there could be humanism, atheism, and all sort of isms—nobody would believe anything unless it could be proved. And where would that leave me?

René D—too clever by half if you ask me.

November 9, 1660

A trip to the New World, as people still insist on calling it—I knew it long before the tourists discovered it. It's bringing in shiploads of visitors these days; I just hope they don't spoil it. It's certainly a land of opportunity, particularly as the Europeans are squabbling for supremacy in both hemispheres. A hefty dose of conflict is always good for business, and both north and south continents are ripe for colonization and exploitation. My only worry is that America might not be attracting the right kind of people: the transatlantic package companies really don't care who they deal with, and a few years ago the Mayflower charter group brought over a positively dreadful bunch of pilgrims. Worse, they have settled here in New England, and the immigrants make no effort to fit in with the local customs and employment laws. What is the world coming to?

Time for stricter immigration control?

THE INTERNATIONAL MARKET

Free Trade agreements oil
the wheels of commerce

November 11, 1660

A good turkey dinner with friends in the South has done a
lot to restore my faith in human nature. The plantations are
a model of how things can be done, and my hosts have an
admirable grasp of modern employment practices: not only
can they exploit the climate (which is damn pleasant, even
in winter), but they have also introduced labor relations
legislation to ensure a constant supply of human resources
from abroad, using reciprocal arrangements with their
colleagues in Africa. Needless to say, I have been personally
involved in the dealing, to make sure that I don't miss out
on any of the action. It's all grist for the mill!

August 17, 1671

I do wish Milton had consulted me before publishing *Paradise Regained*. I am supposed to be his agent, after all. As a sequel to *Paradise Lost*, it's a complete failure. Although it's broadly what we agreed, and makes a good few digs at Big G's shortcomings, he's pushed his luck this time. Anybody reading this would think I was overly ambitious and guilty of hubris—and he's made too much of some of my minor setbacks. I see myself more as a heroic figure, constantly struggling toward ultimate victory, which is how I came across in the first book. I shall have to have words with him.

Am I being too harsh on JM? I mean, he's a nice guy and I'd hate to lose him

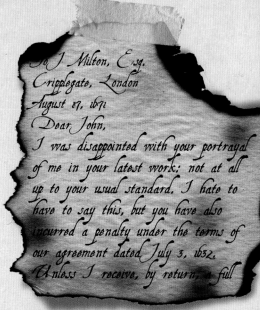

To J Milton, Esq.
Cripplegate, London
August 17, 1671
Dear John,
I was disappointed with your portrayal of me in your latest work: not at all up to your usual standard. I hate to have to say this, but you have also incurred a penalty under the terms of our agreement dated July 3, 1632.
Unless I receive, by return, a full

Salem '93. Drama in the court

May 25, 1693

Good news from the counterintelligence section in New
England: our double agents, working undercover in the
Puritan (pah!) community, have managed to subvert their
religious fervor. There's an old saying in Massachusetts that
"possession is nine parts of the law," and this gave them the
initial idea—once they'd possessed a few impressionable
teenagers, the rest was easy. Mass hysteria ensued, and
within no time the courts were overrun with accusations
of witchcraft. Now my boys are seen as pillars of the local
brotherhood, and appointed as Witchfinders. Who said
these Americans don't appreciate irony?

I'm forever bursting bubbles

October 1, 1720

It's just too easy sometimes. People are so greedy and gullible that I don't have to bother too much. If I had known, I would have got into share trading ages ago. As it happens, I was dead right to set up stock exchanges last century. It's a bit like running the bank at a casino. Spread a few judicious rumors, about the profitability of South Sea company for instance, and investors lose millions. Everybody's looking to do some insider trading, and who do you think they turn to for advice? If I could persuade people to invest heavily in assets that depend on the value of some entirely unrelated thing I could cause financial chaos. Hey, I've just invented derivatives! Now I just have to wait for someone to found Baring's Bank.

Why is it called "filthy" lucre?

The Masonic Temple—
Lodge a complaint

May 12, 1776

Invited to the inaugural meeting of the "Hellfire Club"
in the City of London—if only all secret societies could
be like that! A refreshing change from the Freemasons
who, despite all the hoopla when they got going a couple
of years ago, turned out
to be tiresomely worthy.
No wine, women, and
song, and until I showed
them who was really
Grand Master, they didn't
even notice the potential
for corrupt practices.
A delightful evening of
debauchery today though,
quite exhausting. And so,
to bed.

The George
and Vulture, London—
highly recommended

June 10, 1751

To London again, for an exhibition of prints by my
old friend Hogarth. After drinks with him at his club
[the Hellfire: see previous entry], we make our way to
the gallery. His pictures are a revelation—I had no idea
London was such a lively city! I thought it was only the
gentry who drank to excess like that, but H has captured
some charming scenes of depravity and neglect amongst
the lower classes. Alas, the critics have got the wrong idea,
and see his work as being an indictment rather than a
celebration of street life. But as I told him, it is the lot of
the artist to be misunderstood.

Another few signatures for my collection!

July 4, 1776

All systems go in America. The Revolutionary War is
underway, and today the rebels signed a Declaration of
Independence. On balance, I think this is probably the
way forward, giving me more options among all the power
struggles. Could revolution work in my favor elsewhere
too ... France maybe? The aristocracy aren't exactly popular
there, and I'm sure the peasants could be tempted, given
the right leadership. Maybe even instigate a reign of terror.
Still, I must be careful it doesn't lead to democracy—
although surely there's no danger of that in America.

June 7, 1794

I was right about France: their revolution has
been even better than the Americans'—who
have become disappointingly virtuous since
independence. Working with the Marquis de
Sade was enough to convince me that the
French have a real taste for this sort of
thing, and aren't above seeking my help at
the drop of a hat (or, more to the point,
a head). He started the ball rolling while
he was in prison in the Bastille, and
from then on it was almost too easy.
I was inundated by summonses—

Robespierre, Danton, Marat, and Louis XVI and
Marie Antoinette, just about everybody in
fact. In the end, I just let them fight it out
for themselves, and Madame Guillotine took
care of most of them, under the supervision of
the 'tricoteuses', my agents in France. Robespierre's
in charge, for the moment at least, but
I'm keeping my options open.

You can't have your
cake and eat it,
Marie A. Not now,
anyway

"No pain, no
gain" (M de S).
Whatever turns
you on

Might come
in handy...

...for interpersonal
bonding sessions

December 17, 1798

You win some, you lose some. I have to admit, the revolution idea didn't work in Britain. A flash in the pan, and fun while it lasted, but ancient history now. Anyway, Cromwell was far too incorruptible (those English are so damned polite!), so it's probably just as well they've restored a monarchy with a history of mental instability.

Nevertheless, in case they get too complacent there, I've got their prime minister, William Pitt (his father pulled a few strings from my offices), to introduce Income Tax. This is certainly one of my best schemes yet, and will, I hope, be adopted worldwide. Thank goodness I remembered to set up my own legal and accounting department first, and they advised on how to include loopholes. Of course this sort of information is available to other businesses, and my advisers would be happy to help—at a price.

COMPANY OF
INCORPORATED
SATANIC
ENTERPRISES

Accounts for the tax year
1798–1799

*Certified as a true record of
the Corporation's financial
transactions by*

B. L. Z. Bubb, Esq., auditor

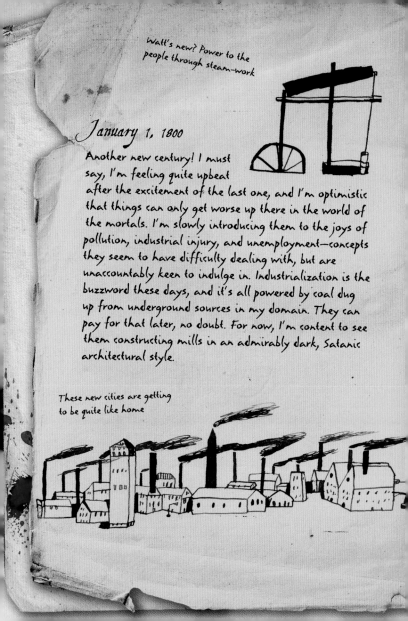

Watt's new? Power to the people through steam-work

January 1, 1800

Another new century! I must say, I'm feeling quite upbeat after the excitement of the last one, and I'm optimistic that things can only get worse up there in the world of the mortals. I'm slowly introducing them to the joys of pollution, industrial injury, and unemployment—concepts they seem to have difficulty dealing with, but are unaccountably keen to indulge in. Industrialization is the buzzword these days, and it's all powered by coal dug up from underground sources in my domain. They can pay for that later, no doubt. For now, I'm content to see them constructing mills in an admirably dark, Satanic architectural style.

These new cities are getting to be quite like home

March 10, 1805

An interesting encounter with a young musician today,
having trouble with diabolical reviews and a serious
substance and gambling habit. The boy can really play,
but I'm not sure the world is ready for a virtuoso banjo
player, so advised him to stick to guitar, or better still
violin. He's ambitious, and has visions of becoming a
solo superstar—and with me as his manager, I can see
no problems. He's got the looks, and loads of charisma,
so should do well with the young female audience in
particular. The stage name's good too, with
a hint of the bad-boy Latin-lover image
the fans are looking for: Niccolò Paganini.
I like it. Signed him up on the spot.

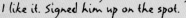

Shake, rattle, and
roll to the beat of
the Danse Macabre

"Monarch of all I survey," or "The Emperor's New Clothes" by W Blake

August 12, 1827

This year's lifetime achievement award has to go to William Blake, even if his work is still woefully misunderstood by the public at large. His arrival here this evening prompted cheers and applause from my staff, and a short acceptance speech from the man himself (although I'm not sure why he had to drag Jerusalem into it). He deserves immortality for those satirical cartoons of Big G alone, but to have written all that comic verse too is quite an accomplishment. Well done, my good and faithful servant!

March 22, 1832

Here we go again. The tired old Faust story gets churned out by any hack writer who can't think of a decent plot for themselves. This time it's Goethe, who was pretty desperate when he called on me back in, ooh, it must have been about 1770. I told him then that he didn't have the talent for the job but he wouldn't take no for an answer, and I suppose portraying me as a loser is his way of getting back at me—but I'll have the last laugh, now he's turned up on my doorstep to pay his dues, and he can spend the rest of eternity watching his "masterpiece" being ignored. I'm getting mighty fed up being summoned by mediocrities who won't take my advice.

Writer's block— brings in the clients, but is it worth it?

November 24, 1859

Can this be the final nail in the coffin of Mr. High and Almighty's masterplan? *The Origin of Species* went on sale this morning, and is selling like hot cakes. In it, I—or at least Darwin, who prepared the final draft in return for a round-the-world trip—have fabricated a totally plausible alternative to the biased reporting of Big G's followers. Basically what I'm saying, sorry, what Darwin is saying, is that humans have evolved by natural selection, and that HE is powerless to do anything about it. Convincing stuff, I thought. Mind you, they still think electricity's the power of the future—if they believe that, they'll believe anything.

SURVIVAL OF THE FITTEST

G's big secret is that when he created man in his image, he ended up with the guy on the left. I helped him set this straight.

Volume V

Towards the Millennium

....

(The Modern World)

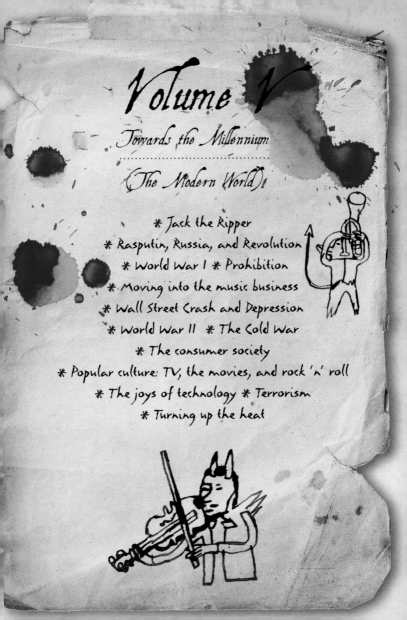

* Jack the Ripper
* Rasputin, Russia, and Revolution
* World War I * Prohibition
* Moving into the music business
* Wall Street Crash and Depression
* World War II * The Cold War
* The consumer society
* Popular culture: TV, the movies, and rock 'n' roll
* The joys of technology * Terrorism
* Turning up the heat

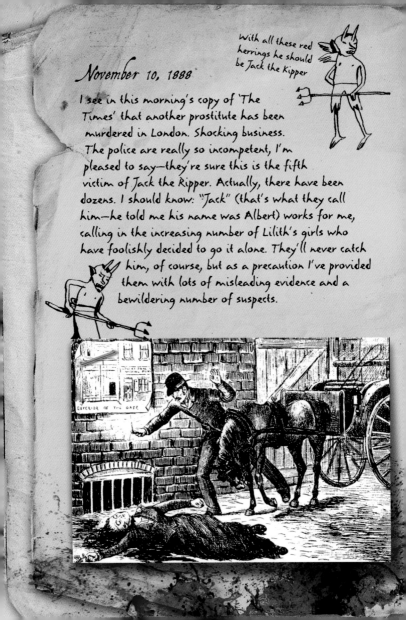

With all these red herrings he should be Jack the Kipper

November 10, 1888

I see in this morning's copy of 'The Times' that another prostitute has been murdered in London. Shocking business. The police are really so incompetent, I'm pleased to say—they're sure this is the fifth victim of Jack the Ripper. Actually, there have been dozens. I should know: "Jack" (that's what they call him—he told me his name was Albert) works for me, calling in the increasing number of Lilith's girls who have foolishly decided to go it alone. They'll never catch him, of course, but as a precaution I've provided them with lots of misleading evidence and a bewildering number of suspects.

November 2, 1889

Every home should have one

I'm quite pleased with the way the telephone has caught on so quickly. The legal wrangles over who owns the patents are still rumbling on, giving me the opportunity to set up a holding company, Associated Terror and Trauma (AT&T, that's got a nice ring to it), to control all further developments. Some of my company's innovations have already come into use—the wrong number, crossed lines, and the busy tone for instance—but the R&D (Research and Disruption) Department has some great ideas for future irritations: automated answering services, helplines, call centers, and cell phones that only ring in theaters.

Telephone sales, courtesy calls … the possibilities are endless

My engineers are trained to deal with important calls

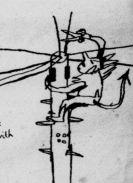

The lunatic's running the asylum now. Ra Ra Rasputin!

April 9, 1905

Had the great pleasure of informing Rasputin that his training period is now over, and he is to report to Tsar Nicholas II as medical adviser. He was delighted to get out of Siberia at last (a most inhospitable place; I must remember that for the future), and put his talents to good use. It's the notoriety that appeals to him, I think, but I haven't the heart to tell him his days are numbered. He's quite mad of course, like most monks, but his influence on the royal family should finally convince the Bolsheviks it's time for a revolution. With any luck, they'll set up a godless republic and inspire other Communist revolts.

September 11, 1911

Curse that Ambrose Bierce! *The Devil's Dictionary*
indeed—what does he know? He's been ripping off
my stuff for years, and now has the nerve to publish
the collected jottings under his own name. It's blatant
plagiarism, and using our trade name in the title is
possibly a breach of company law, too. I'll get the Legal
Department on it. If only he'd come to me first; I'm
sure we could have come to some sort of arrangement.

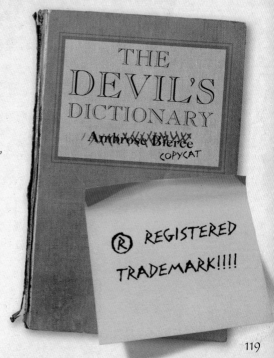

The offending
article. Gives new
meanings to the
words "copyright,"
"original," and
"moral rights"

I almost feel sorry for the guys in the trenches. (Sympathy from the Devil!)

August 4, 1914

Governments can be so touchy, can't they? Not that I mind—it does make life easier for me, but things get a bit out of hand sometimes. Take this year, for instance: in June, I suggested a student prank in Sarajevo, just a small bomb and a lesser aristocrat, and suddenly all Hell breaks loose—name-calling and accusations, and before you know what's going on, there's a World War. A satisfactory result, sure, but not what I had in mind. Still, I'll just let them get on with it now and take a vacation. They seem to be doing quite well without my help.

More explosive than I'd bargained for

BOMB

Old friends come
to enjoy the fun
of a sinking ship

October 26, 1917

You can have too much of a good thing. The war's
been going on for three years now, and they reached
a stalemate ages ago—normally I'm all for a bit of
mindless slaughter, but this one's not my baby and it's
getting in the way of other things. I've tried to hurry
things along a bit, introducing trenchfoot, mustard gas,
and influenza, and as a last resort getting America
to join in too, but it could still take a while. My boy
Lenin was really pissed that nobody had noticed
the revolution in Russia, and refuses to play any
more. I think he's got a point.

Masks—all the rage in Europe these
days, to go with the trenchcoat

Temptation, twenties-style

January 16, 1920

Things have settled down in the last couple of years, and my motto for the new decade is "Let the good times roll!" Naturally, I don't mean that people should just enjoy this period of prosperity willy-nilly—where's the fun in that? No, I've had a much better idea. In my experience, it's been human nature since Adam and Eve to enjoy something more when it's forbidden. So: Prohibition. Easy enough to get the dumb politicians to think it's a good plan, and from now on half the population will be blind drunk most of the time, and the other half either trying to stop them or making a fortune illicitly supplying the stuff. The business opportunities are endless.

March 10, 1928

I've always thought of my business as a service industry, and it looks like the world is catching up with my way of thinking. The big corporations are cashing in, keeping my Banking and Stockbroking Divisions busy, but they need to cover their asses* too. Luckily, I can offer the benefit of our expertise in that area: our legal firms have staff trained in the production of small print and impenetrable jargon, and the Insurance Department has pioneered the get-out clause and "Acts of God" excuses. For those companies unfortunate enough to find themselves in court, we can also offer representation at minimal cost with deferred payment. Besides, most of the judges are on our payroll.

[* Possibly a slip of the pen. I believe he means "assets."]

```
MEMO TO LEGAL DEPARTMENT:
. . . . . . . . . . . . . . . . . . . . . . . . . . . .
Sales and Marketing are planning a major
campaign in the major corporations. Please
ensure your contacts in the
judiciary are prepared
for a rash of breach-of-
contract cases.
```

Order in the court

February 5, 1929

An extended holiday in the Southern
USA. Despite some of the setbacks of the last century, the
Deep South still has a lot to commend it. The folks here are
so gentlemanly, and have quaint ceremonies conducted in
immaculate hoods and gowns. Today I was in New Orleans
for the Mardi Gras celebrations. Fascinating. The Afro-
American community have really got into the swing of
things—I thought the jazz band playing "the Devil's music"
was in my honor, but apparently it goes on all the time
down here, along with voodoo, illegal liquor, and soul food.

Louis and the cats celebrate
our record contract

RJ was very happy with
NP's tips—until I pointed
out "happy" is not really
the sound we're looking for

June 21, 1929

A stroll this evening with
my old friend and house
guest Paganini. Mississippi
is so damned pleasant at this
time of year. At the crossroads we met up with Robert
Johnson. Poor soul—he'd give anything to play the
guitar! Once the paperwork had been completed, P was
persuaded (he owes me a favor or two) to part with a
few tricks of the trade.

October 23, 1929

Time to tidy things up
among the financiers.
I think I'll call in a few
Wall Street contracts.
I don't believe they are
taking me seriously—
some of them seem to
think they can wriggle
out of this deal like they do their own pathetic manmade
scams. Have put Greed* on the job (awfully reliable unless
distracted by anything shiny)—he's so inexplicably popular
up there, they just seem to play into his hands.

October 29, 1929

Result! Eleven of the small-print dodgers in one day.
They're looking pretty sorry for themselves down in Circle
Four, but like I say, what goes up must come down. Greed
says he didn't have to do too much, just have a word with
someone called Dow Jones, et voilà. Sometimes I think it's
all too easy.

[*Mammon, one of the Dark Lord's most trusted demons.]

february 14, 1931

I think I'm suffering from Depression. I'm not the only one, but it's no consolation. It was all going so well: Stock Market crash, widespread poverty, and the Mob running most of the big cities. I had high hopes for the Chicago office, but I regret giving Al Capone the franchise—he showed promise with that reception on Valentine's Day a couple of years ago, then he lets me down with his book-keeping for chrissakes. I told him, speakeasies and gambling are one thing, but you gotta play it clever with the Infernal* Revenue Service, play the system, grease a few palms. Does he listen? Now he's facing a stretch in the Pen. That's sloppy. I'm disappointed. I don't like it when my boys are sloppy. And they don't like it when I'm disappointed.

[* Probably another slip of the pen.]

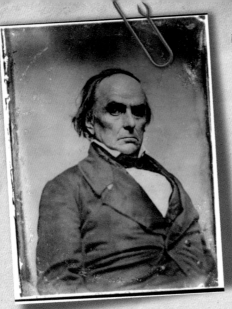

Perhaps I should spread a few juicy rumors myself. Heard the one about Daniel Webster and the goat?

May 15, 1938

I've had to rake the Press Office over the coals again today. There's been another leak.

We all make mistakes, but I rely on them to cover things up for me. Somehow, the 'Saturday Evening Post' got hold of the story of my embarrassing tangle with Daniel Webster, and now everybody's having a good laugh at my expense. The culprit turned out to be a demon called Screwtape, whose nephew Wormwood is an apprentice tempter—with a big mouth and small brain. Uncle S confessed to having told blabbermouth the Webster story, and worse—he sends regular letters to the airhead W advising him how to deal with a prospective client, a Mr. CS Lewis, who is (get this) a columnist for an English newspaper trying to make it as a children's writer. I'll have to see if I can get the Screwtape Letters back before they get published, too.

March 10, 1940

Bad business, all the negative publicity
I've been getting lately. Good thing I
got Mikhail Bulgakov on the copy-
writing team to redress the balance—
he's already got a good track record,
and I like Russian writers (Dostoevsky
and Goncharov in particular understood
what I wanted from them). His brief was to improve my
image a bit, which he has done better than I could have
hoped. Bulgakov's 'The Master and Margarita' is simply
a factual account of my visit to the USSR, woven in with
a bit of background stuff about Pontius Pilate, and a
convincing love story where I get the girl for a change.
I don't normally like happy endings, but this one works.

All in all, I'm delighted with
the book, and only sorry
that I had to call in his debt
before he had a chance to
enjoy the royalties. Business
is business.

Samizdis, samizdat—
any enemy of Joe
Stalin's a friend
of mine

This scam may be more successful than the BLACK MARKET

Don't Let That Shadow Touch Them
Buy WAR BONDS

December 8, 1941

They're at it again—and without my help once more. This is not at all the way to go about things. I blame that little upstart Schicklgruber* or whatever he calls himself these days. He had a few good ideas when we first met at his painting and decorating business, but he wouldn't listen to a word I said, and insisted on going it alone. I thought they'd keep it a local affair this time, but it's snowballed and the unfortunate misunderstanding at Pearl Harbor has got everybody hot under the collar. It'll all end in tears.

[*Adolf Hitler]

February 20, 1950

They're having a witch hunt! Oh, that takes me back. It's led by that bullshitting bourbon-guzzling little weasel from Wisconsin, Joe McCarthy. We did a deal in the '30s: I got him his law degree in one year on the usual terms, but we were so busy after 1945 I forgot all about the little runt. He's been doing OK in a low-end kinda way—spreading lies about his war record and the kind of filthy rumors about everybody else that netted a good few suicides—but this is a high-profile triumph, and he's gunning for Hollywood lefties, so he can't lose. Means I'll get down to La La land, check out the laydeez, mix a bit of work and pleasure....

Bummer. Been looking over the files, and apparently I can't claim this one. It was Roman Catholic priest Edmund Walsh who came up with the whole commie-bashing Red Scare thing for McCarthy.

March 1, 1954

IT WASN'T ME*. They did it all by themselves.
Shows you what happens when geeks breed. They have
just "tested" another H-bomb, but failed to do the math,
duh, and it went off louder and bigger than they thought.
Just wait til I get them down here. One atoll vaporized,
marine life obliterated, nuclear fallout all over the Pacific
for the next few millennia, 264 people irradiated but,
and more importantly, serious structural damage in the
Eighth Circle, which means I've got to find somewhere
else to store the fraudsters, liars, and corrupt politicians!
Logistical nightmare. And the Four Horsemen have woken
up and put themselves on red alert, which always makes
them insufferable.

[* This must refer to the second U.S. H-bomb test at Bikini Atoll in the Pacific.
It was a 15 megaton bomb and the biggest manmade explosion ever, until the
Soviets went one better in 1961.]

October 28, 1962

In retrospect, I think I was right to step in in 1945. The whole world was working for the war effort, and my operatives found themselves with nothing to do. Just as well the Technical Department kept busy though—they came up with the bomb that brought them all to their senses, stopping all the asinine fighting and restoring a global atmosphere of mutual distrust. Of course, they all want one now, and there's a healthy arms race running along with the Cold War. Only this week there was a Mexican standoff in Cuba, but they haven't cottoned on to the fact that I pull the strings on both sides now. Well, we have to protect our interests, too. Upping the number of nuclear states would seem to be the way forward: we're working on a couple of refinements for smaller client states already, and continuing to improve products for our existing customers. Polaris sales remain steady, but I'm pushing for a new generation of missiles of my own design. I think Trident would be an appropriate name, wouldn't it?

To Production Manager—is this the right warning symbol for radioactive substances?

*Dallas '63, from the depot
security camera. Nothing
unusual to report*

♆ November 22, 1963

A tedious exercise in Texas today. The Publications
Department asked me to oversee a surprise inspection of
security in our Dallas book repository, following reports
of a suspicious character on the grassy knoll opposite.
As I was examining one of the guns, the blasted thing
went off. Luckily I emerged unscathed, but to my great
pleasure it caused a commotion in the street outside.

April 5, 1965

They'll swallow anything, that lot. Not content with swilling down any fizzy sugar-water our subsidiary companies can churn out, so long as it's got a "secret recipe," the Catering Division have discovered they'll pay through the nose for the processed gunk coming out of our intensive agriculture experiments as waste product. "Fast food" they call it, presumably because of the speed it whips through the digestive system. Or maybe it's because we can only sell the worst of the stuff to airlines. There's no accounting for taste, I suppose, and if that's what the new consumer society wants, I'm happy to go on supplying it. But I do think the mortals are getting things a bit too easy these days, which is why I've brought in a few packaging innovations, building on the success of the sardine and corned beef cans with the keys that went missing and the jagged edges that result when you open them. The cardboard milk carton (so hard to pour—and not easy to open, heh heh!) has been a resounding success, and field trials are in progress for impossible to self assemble self-assembly furniture and a range of unreliable kitchen gadgets and hazardous do-it-yourself power tools. That's what I call progress.

Remind Finance Dept. to buy shares in Band Aid

My kind of town—I could be big here

HOLLYWOOD

June 12, 1968

Word of mouth, that's the way to do business. Look where it's got me now—Hollywood! Ira Levin gets writer's block, I give him a couple of ideas (usual terms, of course): one satisfied customer. He tells his friend Polanski, who contacts me, and before you know it we've got a blockbuster on our hands. I'm guest of honor at the premiere of 'Rosemary's Baby' (a touching romantic comedy), and meeting all sorts of movie moguls looking for advice on future projects. I've already got them signed up for a biopic of an exorcist, and I'm negotiating the rights of a series of films about an antichrist. Polanski introduced me to these guys—I reckon it's a good omen.

It's not the stars that make the money, it's The Producers. Ask Mel Brooks

Screenplay? Child's play!

June 13, 1968

Much as I love the movie business, you still can't beat a good book. Hollywood's got the glitz, but they'd be nowhere without good writers. Although I've got fingers in a lot of pies in Tinsel Town, I see myself as more of a literary agent really—and with authors like Dennis Wheatley on my books, the film rights are an added bonus. He's getting on a bit now though, and I need someone to take his place... a promising student contacted me only the other day about cheating on his final exams, and he told me he'd written some short stories. King, I think his name was. I'll look him up.

MEMO TO SELF

. . . .

Drop in to University of Maine on way home. Draw up revised contracts in name of "King, Stephen."

A shining example of how to carry out business

Lennon says The Beatles are bigger than Jesus. Yeah, but not bigger than me!

December 31, 1968

A funny sort of year. Things were going well in Vietnam, but that seems to be fizzling out now. The only consolation is that we've managed to get our latest signing, Nixon, into the White House. I had hoped for a youth movement in my favor too, with that nice Manson family and all the illicit substances brought back by the Armed Forces, but even this has gone sour on me—the hippies hijacked it and we got "flower power," "Summer of Love," and other nonsense. What's wrong with young people today?

"Make Love, Not War," "Peace and Love." This generation's got some f-upped priorities

I always knew my boys
would look stunning
in leather

December 6, 1969

My faith in human nature has been restored. After the
disappointment of the "Peace and Love" era (short-lived,
I'm happy to say), young people have reverted to type.
No more pretty little tunes—rock and heavy metal are
the order of the day now, and the disaster of Woodstock
this August has been mitigated by the wonderful show
at Altamont. I confess I had a hand in events there, to
move things along a little and ensure all ran smoothly
(M Jagger wrote a lovely song expressing his gratitude
and sympathy); and although I can't officially sanction
the Club, I condone their actions and broadly support their
aims and objectives. Well done boys!

Drum sets—my special gift to moms and dads everywhere!

August 9, 1974

Technology. I just love it—especially sound recording, which has so many useful applications: maddeningly anodyne piped music in public places (elevators, shopping malls, hotel lobbies, dentists' offices, public bathrooms, you name it), or over the phone to callers put on hold (almost indefinitely); canned laughter on TV sitcoms and badly dubbed movie soundtracks ... I could go on. But the crowning glory has to be the historic recordings of a virtuoso performance by Richard Nixon, just released as "The Watergate Tapes." A masterpiece of comic timing.

Recording the laugh-track for the Nixon tapes

Note: this guy wants further meetings—asked if I had any Windows in the 1990s

This is the future. And doesn't it look good?!

November 28, 1975

Dinner (if you call a burger and fries dinner) with a truly tedious young man ... the name escapes me now. (Yates? Tates?) Presented me with an incomprehensible MS, detailing plans for something he calls "software." Brilliant of course, but lacking the imagination to see the potential of his ideas—I suggest an annual update for instance, negating all previous issues, and a random shutdown facility. Have agreed to set him up in business (the usual terms), but insist on putting a couple of my people on board—left to his own devices it could all run tiresomely smoothly. Mustn't forget to arrange for bugs in both his software and his offices.

April 30, 1977

Got an invite to the opening of Studio 54 a few days ago—
I am a man of wealth and taste after all!—and I've only
just got back. Fantastic; didn't even have to bother with a
disguise. Really touched that the first vinyl to hit the wheels
of steel was called "Devil's Gun." Aw, you guys. I got a
VIP tour of the Rubber Room, and it was just like the old
days in Gomorrah. And when they brought out the mirrors
and razor blades and $100 bills and a few shitloads of
Charlie—which they're now calling the Devil's Dandruff
but I can't bring myself to sue—I almost shed a tear. It
makes a change to be summoned just for your company.
So of course I stuck around, showed them all how to really
boogie on down, broke a few hearts, cut some great deals
on a lot of souls; it was hard to tear myself away. I'm going
back next Saturday night.

January 1, 1980

Apart from disco, the '70s sucked; all we get these days are drugged-out old hippies who don't even know they're here (and if I hear one more 50-minute guitar solo, I'll eat my own head), deluded old warmongers who think it's just another part of Nam, and eviled-out old world dictators who think they run the place. Enough already! This is going to be My Decade! It's gonna be all about money, style, bling, fast cars, hot chicks in short skirts, and Me, Me, Me! No more getting medieval. Greed has come up with a great rebrand concept and business strategy for himself, Vanity, Envy, and Lust, and a killer tagline: Greed is Good. I like it. He's got a seven-year plan (those Commies were good for something) that will guarantee regular delivery of arrogant, ruthless assholes who will really make the joint jump, and be pleased to see me. I can't wait.

Lunch is for wimps

September 1989

What a ride! Aside from a few inevitable outbreaks of Do Goodery (Live Aid!), this decade has been such a blast that I've been neglecting my diary. Who'd have thought the little free-willers would have become such pushovers? His market share is in freefall. (Mind you, Greed is getting a bit uppity.*)

REMEMBER TO CULTIVATE SOME NEW HABITS

* MEMO TO SELF. WATCH GREED, HE'S AFTER A CORNER OFFICE. AND SOME. SHUNT HIM SIDEWAYS? WILL HE FALL FOR BIT OF SLICK UPTITLING, IF I CAN GET VANITY ON SIDE?

[a continuation of previous entry]

I've been talking to some of the hedge-fund burnouts when they're on a break from the scorpion pit, and they've been telling me about corporate raiding. So I've just signed up this guy Steven R Covey, who's written a book all about helping yourself to everything*, full of ideas about how to shaft the opposition that are so advanced even Machiavelli was impressed. The author gets the usual obscene wealth, everlasting fame (for a certain value of everlasting, natch, even he didn't read the small print), and I get to invent a whole raft of diabolical non-jobs (brand strategist, media consultant, time management executive) that will generate a healthy incoming revenue stream to enhance Satancorp's core activities. Dontcha just love this management speak?

[* Probably a reference to *The Seven Habits of Highly Effective People*, first published in 1989, Stephen R Covey.]

My people will talk to your people, but they won't know what the hell they are talking about

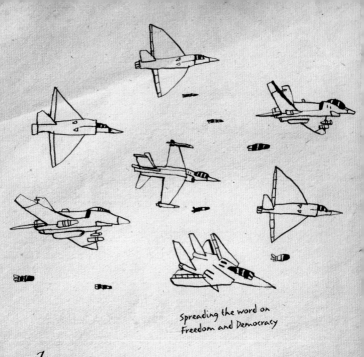

Spreading the word on
freedom and Democracy

January 17, 1991

Things are heating up, and it's a welcome return to
Mesopotamia for me. I'd had enough of all that Cold
War nonsense—particularly with that old fool Reagan
working for me. Okay, he got the Star Wars thing going,
and at least remembered his lines when it came to the
Evil Empire speech, but he got confused about who his
friends were. I mean the Iron Lady was fair enough,
but Gorbachev? I give up. Still, his successor's shaping up
nicely, and has even found a new enemy to play in the
sandpit with. Now where's my address book?

October 23, 1996

Some of my advisers are getting all worked up about the rise of religion again. On the one hand we've got the born-again brigade, on the other the Taliban, and they're worried we might get squeezed out. Fat chance! Don't they remember the Crusades? I'm already on the case: I've secured the services of Osama bin Laden to bring the two sides nicely into conflict and turn all the hype to our advantage. Once the Americans have stopped wasting their time trying to nail my client OJ, I'm sure they can be persuaded to join in the fun.

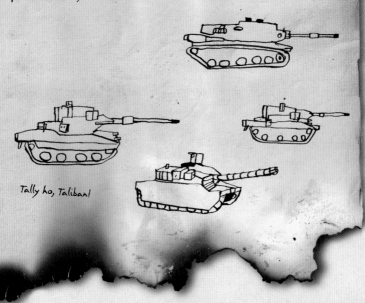

Tally ho, Taliban!

January 26, 1998

Monica, Monica, what a find you turned out to be. Little Miss Innocent with your rosy cheeks and your bouffant hair. You can bite the end off my cigar any time you like. "I did not have sexual relations with that woman, Miss Lewinsky." Ha! Our agents Tripp and Starr really earned their performance bonuses with this one. Of course, Slick Willie's not the first "Leader of the Free World" (do they really still say that?) to have problems keeping it zipped up, but caught red-handed on prime-time TV? Second term screwed, impeachment, scandal, Gore and his puritanical views on climate change kept well away from the White House (actually that turned out to be more of a close call than I had bargained for, and good ol' Jeb is going to be calling in the favors big time when he gets down here), and that bossy know-it-all Hillary holed beneath the waterline for 2009. It's days like this that make the job worthwhile.

It started with a kiss...

December 31, 1999

It being the Millennium, I suppose I ought to be making some apocalyptic New Year's resolutions, even though Big G doesn't seem to have got the Second Coming organized yet. So, here goes:

Short-term
• At the stroke of midnight, press the Y2K button on my laptop. I'll give them a Second Coming!
• Buy more shares in Enron: it looks likes it's going places
• Raise oil prices

Medium-term
• Step up email advertising campaigns, including the personal organ enhancement scheme and the "business opportunities" offered by our Nigerian office
• Find a good lawyer for S Milosevic
• Stir things up in the Middle East, especially Iraq and Iran (try to remember which is which)
• Appoint a good campaign manager for the Bush boy (don't worry about Russia: our Vlad's a shoo-in)

Long-term
• Be more lavish in my sponsoring of terrorism
• Precipitate (good word!) further climate change

March 20, 2003

It's just like old times, being back in Babylon again. Baghdad's changed quite a bit, for the better I think, although the whole place needs a shake-up—a regime change is as good as a rest. George W's the best I could find, unfortunately, and he's convinced he's doing Big G's work (or following in Daddy's footsteps), on the pretext that Goddam Hussein's got WMD. If only. He's turned out to be a real disappointment, and I'm not going to help him a second time. There are plenty of other fish in the sea, now we've organized the Axis of Evil!

Can you see any weapons?
No, neither can I....

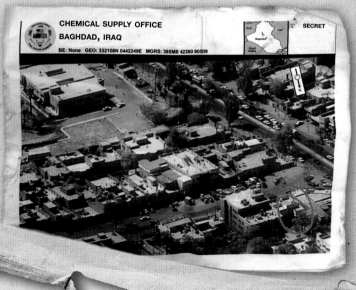

CHEMICAL SUPPLY OFFICE
BAGHDAD, IRAQ

SECRET

BE: None   GEO: 332108N 0442249E   MGRS: 38SMB 42360 90509

September 5, 2003

Martha Stewart's going down! I've been trying to get her off my back ever since we did the deal. She's a forceful dame; insisted on inspecting the premises, and before I could stop her she had feng-shui'd* the Third Circle; color-coordinated the red-hot pokers; covered the Boiling Oil Department with matching doilies, oven mitts, and aprons; and had the handcarts painted a nice blue. And don't talk to me about the distressed cloisonné shit tongs. The plan is she will repent, He'll be contractually obliged to take her in, then they'll be her glue-gunning lackeys for eternity. It's a good thing. Ha!

* MEMO TO SELF: FENG SHUI IS A NICE LITTLE EARNER, THOUGH; PASS IT ON TO THE FOOLS/ MONEY BOYS IN THE ACCOUNTANCY PIT?

The last thing this place needs is a woman's touch

OK, I'm sorry, maybe I did go a bit far in this instance

September 13, 2004

Time for a review of the music scene. Dear God. Jazz and rock'n'roll and Blues and reggae, all pretty straightforward stuff—get drunk, rebel, sleep around, ignore your elders and betters, keep up your narcotic intake. Delivers a steady stream of sinners. But what have we had lately? Britney and J-Lo and Mariah ululate along in a syrup of over-produced synth, although I suppose they persuade large quantities of young women to focus on shaking their booty rather than that tedious hairy feminist stuff that was threatening to shake things up dangerously a few years ago. But the award for anesthetizing the masses with banal, mind-emptying shlock goes to the best-selling female singer in the world. Step forward Celine Dion, the singing horse, undeniably a work of mine, although I reserve the right not to listen, no matter how long her heart goes on, and on, and on, and on . . .

November 10, 2004

I know I'm not supposed to say this, but Christianity has
a lot going for it as a means of furthering our base, corrupt,
and (let's hear it for Team Beelzebub!) downright evil
enterprise. The Bible Belt is alive and well, but of course
none of these knuckleheads get G's point about caring for
the poor and spreading peace and love and mercy and all
that stuff. All they care about is sex. So teaching children
that G made the birds and the bees is more important than
teaching them about the birds and the bees (highest teenage
pregnancy rate in the Western world anyone?). "Abortion
is a greater threat to human survival than climate change,"
"gay sex is a more odious affront to society than child
poverty." You can't make this shit up. G is hopping about
in the Heavenly heights trying to figure out where it has
all gone wrong, while his loyal cohorts do my job for me.
I wish I'd thought of religion.

Come and try it down here!
There's a lot of fun to be
had. . . .

January 30, 2006

A brief trip upstairs to congratulate one of our longest-serving executives on officially becoming a senior citizen. Not that he shows any sign of retiring, no sir, Richard Bruce Cheney has a lot of miles left in him yet. I remember those early drunk-driving, draft-dodging years and little thought then what a pillar of our operation he would become. Just look at his record. He's worked for Nixon, Rumsfeld, Ford, and Bushes pappy and sonny. He voted against releasing that international life-affirming treasure Mandela. He headed a vice-presidential selection committee that selected himself. He has managed to neuter most of the Congressional laws brought in to control the President after that jerk Nixon blew his cover. And to top it all he has promoted a war that has generated millions of dollars for his own company. Hats off I say, and God Bless America.

One of our own

DIABOLICAL GREETINGS

You want ice with that? Too bad

February 16, 2007

Is it hot in here or is it just me? Ha, just my little joke.
A non-binding agreement signed in Washington today
apparently concedes that climate change is happening and
that something maybe might have to be done about it
by someone, though probably not us but them over there,
and probably not now but in 2012 when the provisions
of Kyoto 1997 have been fulfilled. According to my little
crew of weathermen, four countries have a chance of
meeting their CO_2 targets. Four! The phrase "to hell in a
handbasket" springs to mind. And, of course, my sources
in India and China say they have no intention of going
back to donkeys and bicycles while the US citizenry eat,
drink, and breathe gasoline. The Four Horsemen have
muttered darkly about missing out on their promised
Apocalypse, but it will save me a lot in fees and expenses
if the human race can be persuaded simply to drown
themselves. I'll need to build an extension.
And what will G say then, huh?

September 4, 2007

That low-life Cheney! A rumor's going round that there's
going to be an extraordinary Board Meeting called to
discuss our corporate strategy. Corporate strategy my ass.
I know what this is about. I went down to chat with the
stokers earlier on since they always have their irons in the
fire. Seems like the Four Horsemen are getting antsy again
and regard "regime change" as the way forward, so there's
going to be a leveraged buyout with executives from Enron,
Fox News International, and Microsoft raising the funds
on some kind of private equity basis. And Cheney's lined
up to be the new CEO when he gets here next year. I made
him what he is today and this is how he repays me? Oh I
know, after however many millennia it's been, you should
know not to trust anybody, but I really thought Cheney
was a kindred spirit. Well he needn't think he's getting

Whatever happens,
I'm keeping tabs on
my trust fund

[a continuation of previous entry]

his hands on all this. I haven't been working my butt off in this sweatbox so that some overweight, dyke-fathering building contractor can swan in and take it off me (by the way, it really is getting a hell of a lot hotter down here). I'll get the boys together and we will see this off. Machiavelli and Milosevic can take care of PR, Capone will do fund-raising, Goebbels can have publicity (we'll need to lock Nixon in his room with his goddamn tape machine). Life in the Old Nick yet, eh? There's someone at the door, I'll have to finish this later....

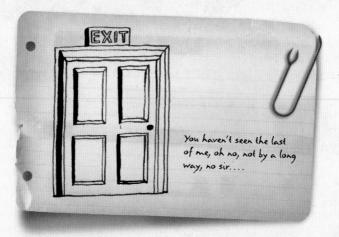

You haven't seen the last of me, oh no, not by a long way, no sir....

[This is the last dated entry in the sheaf of papers given to me by the author's agent; the only other document was an office plan, which I present to you on the following pages. Unfortunately, there is no indication as to the result of the Board Meeting, or indeed any confirmation that it took place. Mr. Cheney's office refused to comment when I contacted them, citing vice-presidential privilege, so I'm afraid that, as they say, the rest is silence. MJW]

My latest office plan

Directory of Departmental Heads

PRESIDENT, CEO, FOUNDER, AND CHAIRMAN OF THE BOARD: Satan [aka Gaap, The Devil, The Dark Lord, Scratch and, to his friends, Old Nick—i.e. my Good Self] ext: 666

VICE PRESIDENT: Mephistopheles ext: 665

DIRECTOR OF HUMAN RESOURCES: Lilith ext: 001

FINANCE DIRECTOR: Mammon [aka Greed] ext: 100 000 000

TRANSPORT MANAGER: Leviathan ext: A2B

HEAD OF PUBLIC RELATIONS: Lucifer ext: 5

PRODUCTION AND ENERGY: Abaddon ext: 0

EXECUTIVE OFFICER, LEGAL DEPARTMENT: Beelzebub ext: 10

BUILDINGS MANAGER: Asmodai [aka Asmodeus]. ext: 4x2

SALES AND MARKETING: Pithius ext: 7734

 CATERING: Moloch ext: 999

 ADVERTISING: Belial ext: 121

 MILITARY LIAISON OFFICER: Berith ext: 54321

 TRAINING AND EDUCATION: Belphegor ext: 1234

 AGRICULTURAL CONSULTANT: Astaroth ext: 333

 PRESS OFFICER: Baal (contact via Fox News or Al Jazeera)

USEFUL CONTACTS

Oval Office hotline 800-650-0000 duby@bush.gov
Pentagon 555-555-5555 world@war.org
D Rumsfeld 800-650-0001 don@unknownknowns.net
D Cheney 999-543-2121 finger@thetrigger.biz
O bin L (cellphone) 0773 491191 still@large.ok
~~S Hussein 122235678~~
V Putin 007 495 0000 (switchboard—ask for "Mr. Big")
vlad@kremlin.info
M Stewart marth@livingdangerously.net
M Gadaffy AliG@daffydux.lib
W of B madam@baghdadbroth.el

Acknowledgments

I should like to thank all those who have assisted in the compilation of this book, whose help and encouragement was invaluable in the mammoth task of editing and preparing the documents for publication. Many, for reasons of their own personal security, cannot be named here (but they will know to whom I am referring). I would like to extend my especial gratitude to the tireless workers in the IV Corporation who did so much to restore and preserve the crumbling codices and decipher the often unintelligible manuscripts; also to the author's agent, M. F. St. Opheles, and his secretary, Ms Persephone Kore. Above all, I must thank the Dark Lord himself, without whose gracious co-operation none of this would have been possible. MJW